Based on the characters
by Robert Rodriguez

Written by Elizabeth Lenhard

HYPERION
MIRAMAX BOOKS
New York

For information address Hyperion Paperbacks for Children,
114 Fifth Avenue, New York, New York 10011-5690.

Printed in the United States of America

First Edition

1 3 5 7 9 10 8 6 4 2

This book is set in 13/17 New Baskerville.

ISBN 0-7868-1718-6

Visit www.spykids.com

CHAPTER 1

The moon was just rising over the quiet city when Carmen and Juni Cortez emerged from the Pseuterian embassy. They paused for a moment at the top of a long swath of marble steps and heaved a couple of big sighs.

"Well," Juni said, unknotting his black silk bow tie, "I guess we did it again."

"Saved the world, you mean?" Carmen said. She was shifting uncomfortably from one foot to the other. Her silk party shoes were *killing* her.

"Well, we saved Pseuteria, anyway," Juni said. He was referring, of course, to the little known but still very important island nation in the middle of the Pacific Ocean. Ever since Pseuteria had been discovered a few years ago, all sorts of power-mad dictators had been trying to take it over. They wanted to get their hands on Pseuteria's vast wealth of natural resources, which included everything from emeralds to oil to a new strain of extrafudgy cocoa beans.

Earlier tonight, yet another crazed criminal named Clarence Kao had plotted to take over the little country. Intelligence sources had reported that he planned to stage a coup during the Pseuterian embassy's annual Diplomats' Ball. There were going to be hostages, ransom demands—the whole nine yards.

And that's why the OSS—the Office of Strategic Services, a top-secret government agency that thwarts evil on a daily basis—had sent Carmen and Juni to head off the disaster.

And who exactly are Carmen and Juni Cortez? They're Spy Kids. That's right. Spies—ages twelve and ten. Spies with amazing gadgetry. Spies with ultracool spy parents. Spies with stylin' cargo pants, gizmo-laden vests, and tricked-out boots.

Well . . . usually.

Tonight, Juni was actually wearing a starched shirt, a too tight tuxedo, and patent-leather dancing shoes. His bouncy red curls were slicked back with tons of hair gel. Carmen wore a pink satin ball gown and long white gloves. Her dark wavy hair was swept up into a dramatic bun on top of her head, and little diamonds sparkled in her earlobes.

The Cortez kids were looking fine.

But they were feeling . . . a little weary.

"I hope the next coup is out in a jungle or in a nice, muddy cave," Juni said. He flopped down on a step halfway down the staircase. "Then we can wear our usual fatigues and crawl around in the dirt. I mean, getting really dirty without getting in trouble is one of the best parts about being a spy!"

Carmen shrugged and nodded her head.

"You're right," she said.

"I am?" Juni blurted. "You hardly ever agree with me."

"I know," Carmen said. She kicked off her pointy shoes and flopped down on the step next to him. She wiggled her pinched toes painfully. "But that party really blew. Everyone was, like, ancient!"

"And *so* boring!" Juni said. "I got stuck trading stock tips with some finance minister for twenty minutes."

"And the food!" Carmen cried. "Did you know that pâté is the smushed-up livers of geese? Gross!"

"Oh, it wasn't so bad," Juni said, puffing out his chest. Juni prided himself on being a connoisseur of all things edible. Even gross things.

"Come off it, Juni," Carmen scoffed. "I saw you spit out that wad of pâté behind the ice sculpture."

"Only because I accidentally mixed it with that fishy beluga caviar," Juni retorted. "*Talk* about gross. Anyway, nobody saw."

"Only because Kao chose just that moment to pull out his hand grenade," his sister replied. "Lucky you!"

Carmen peeled off one of her long satin gloves and eyed the black disk strapped to her hand.

"And *un*lucky Kao," she muttered. "This Swat 'n' Splat got him good!"

She unlooped two elastic straps from her pinkie and thumb and carefully lifted the disk off her palm. Then she nestled the gadget into a special pocket in her purse.

"Be very careful with that Swat 'n' Splat!" Juni warned. "Clearly, Uncle Machete hasn't worked out all its bugs yet."

Machete Cortez was their dad's older brother. He was also the inventor of the Spy Kids' most ingenious gadgets. But genius sometimes comes with a price. Imagine, for instance, X-ray vision contact lenses that turn your eyes lime green. Or rocket shoes that sound like burping ducks.

Or take the Swat 'n' Splat. Uncle Machete had promised that the gizmo would unleash a huge, virtual flyswatter. The swatter was supposed to squish a villain into submission until the Spy Kids could slap their cuffs onto his wrists.

But when Carmen had actually deployed the gadget at the Diplomats' Ball, the virtual flyswatter had melted into a puddle of purple goo. Sure, the goo had taken out Kao. But it had also splattered on many of the well-dressed guests.

"Yeah," Carmen said as she snapped her purse closed. "We saved the day, but it wasn't a *completely* flawless rescue. I hate it when that happens."

"Me, too," Juni said. That was about the only other thing Carmen and Juni could agree on. They were both supercompetitive. They weren't satisfied with a mission unless they'd pulled it off to perfection.

Before they could lapse into a sulkfest, though, the Spy Kids saw something that made them perk up. A sleek, silver SUV pulled up to the curb in front of the embassy.

"Well, at least our *timing* was flawless," Carmen said, pulling herself to her feet. "There's our ride."

The tinted window on the SUV's passenger side slid downward as the Spy Kids trudged down the steps. Their mom waved at them through the open window.

"Mission accomplished?" she asked with a dimpled grin.

"Of course," Juni said, sliding into the SUV's

backseat. He smiled wanly at his dad, who was sitting in the driver's seat. Then, he gave Carmen a sidelong look as she followed him into the car. "There might have been a *couple* of glitches—"

"And *someone* might have coughed up a wad of pâté," Carmen added, giving her brother a teasing glance.

"*But*," Juni added quickly, "the important thing is, we averted the coup. Clarence Kao will never be prime minister of Pseuteria."

"Thanks to our Spy Kids," said Dad proudly. "So tell us, how did you do it this time?"

"Well, Juni picked Kao out of the crowd right away," Carmen explained as she climbed into the car. She pulled her puffy pink skirt into the backseat and shut the car door.

"It was his Pseuterian accent," Juni scoffed. "Totally phony."

"Kao pulled out a hand grenade," Carmen continued, "and I took him down with the Swat 'n' Splat."

"Excellent job," Dad cried in his lilting Spanish accent. "I'm proud of you, Carmenita. In fact, I think both of you kids deserve a reward."

"A reward?" Juni asked wearily. "What, like a day off from training?"

"Or help studying our spy manuals?" Carmen asked wearily.

"I was thinking more like ice-cream sundaes," Dad declared, shifting the SUV into drive. "Big ones!"

"Yay!" the Spy Kids cried.

Twenty minutes later, Carmen and Juni were sitting with their parents in a booth at an old-fashioned ice-cream parlor. They were both digging into mountains of frozen deliciousness.

"Whoo-hoo," Carmen said, admiring her butterscotch sundae. "Extra rainbow sprinkles. That's what I like to see!"

"I haven't had bubble-gum ice cream since I was, like, eight," Juni added, gnawing on some frozen gum balls. "Man, those were the days."

As Juni blew a gigantic, sticky bubble, Mom and Dad exchanged a worried glance.

"What's wrong?" Juni said, sucking in his bubble with a squelching sound.

"Has it really been that long since you had bubble-gum ice cream?" Mom asked. Her sparkly green eyes were crinkled with concern.

"And Carmen," Dad said to his daughter. "When was the last time you stayed up too late, yakking on the phone with your school friends?"

"Um, last time I checked, that was a *bad* thing," Carmen said in confusion. "You *hate* it when I hog the phone."

"Yes, but you're practically a teenager, now," Mom said. "You're supposed to do irritating things like hogging the phone."

"Okay, I'm totally confused," Juni said. "Are you saying you *want* Carmen to be annoying? More annoying than she already *is*?!"

"Juni," Mom said, chiding him gently. "Of course, we're glad that you kids are so responsible. But, well, your father and I were talking about your lives as Spy Kids. And, to tell you the truth, we're a bit worried."

"Worried?" Carmen blurted. "But we're highly trained superspies. We can handle totally dangerous situations."

"I'm a master bomb diffuser," Juni added.

"And I'm a computer hacker extraordinaire," Carmen said.

"Between us, we speak fourteen languages," Juni said. "*And* I can do a mean grand jeté and bake a crème brûlée."

"So," Carmen said with a shrug, "believe us, you have nothing to worry about."

"Of course, that is all fantastic," Dad said. "But

don't you ever wish your childhoods were just a bit more . . . normal?"

"Normal?" Carmen stared at her parents blankly. "You mean, the way we used to be?"

There *had* been a time when the Cortezes had been an average family of four. Mom and Dad had worked at home as consultants. Carmen and Juni had gone to a private elementary school. They'd had a cozy, peaceful life in their mansion on a cliff-top above the ocean.

One fateful day, Carmen and Juni had discovered that their parents were retired spies. In fact, they'd once been the best spies their countries had ever known!

But when Ingrid and Gregorio Cortez had fallen in love, gotten married, and become parents, they'd dropped out of the dangerous spy game. That is, until the day an important mission came their way. The mission had been too juicy to refuse, so Mom and Dad had left their kids with a baby-sitter. Then they'd gone off to save the world.

Of course, all those years out of the spy game had made them a little rusty. No sooner had Mom and Dad begun their mission than they'd gotten into a major jam. That's when Carmen and Juni had become spies themselves—and saved their parents' butts.

Now, the Cortezes worked as a spy family. They were constantly jetting off to exotic places and foiling supervillains with cunning and gadgetry. And yes, occasionally, they had to fight off horrible creatures. Or endure a brief imprisonment.

Still, the Spy Kid life sure beat "normal childhood."

"As far as I can tell," Juni said, taking another bite of his peanut-butter-and-bubble-gum sundae, "'normal' equals 'boring.'"

"I hate to keep agreeing with Juni," Carmen said, "but I agree."

"I bet you'll reconsider that when we tell you our idea," Mom said. She shot Dad a secret grin.

"Idea?" Juni said apprehensively. "What sort of idea?"

"It's almost July," Dad pointed out. "And what do most children do in July?"

"Um . . ."

"They go to summer camp!" Mom blurted with a giddy chortle. "And now, so do you!"

The parents beamed.

The Spy Kids gasped.

"No!" they cried.

CHAPTER 2

"I . . . I don't understand," Dad said. Carmen and Juni were gaping at their parents in distress. They'd even forgotten their half-devoured ice-cream sundaes. "Don't all children want to go to summer camp?"

"But we're not *all* children," Carmen pointed out. "We're Spy Kids."

"Yeah," Juni said with a peanut-butter-smeared pout. "And from what I hear, summer camp is dorky. With sing-alongs."

"And poison ivy," Carmen added.

"And bad food," Juni added.

"And toasted marshmallows," Carmen said, rolling her brown eyes.

"Hey," Juni said. "That part actually sounds kinda good."

"See?" Mom piped up. She reached over the table with a napkin and wiped a bit of whipped cream off Juni's cheek. "I think you'll love camp."

Carmen was pretty sure that she would hate camp. But she didn't say another word. She didn't want to hurt her parents' feelings. They really seemed to be into this whole "normal kid" thing. It must have been some wacky phase they were going through.

Of course, Juni wasn't *quite* as sensitive to Mom's and Dad's feelings as Carmen.

"Camp is lame!" he blurted out. "And besides—what if the world needs saving and we're stuck in arts and crafts making macramé pot holders? That would be even *lamer.*"

"That does it," Dad said, slamming his fist on the table. "Juni, you can't save the world single-handedly. You need to have some fun. You and your sister are *going* to camp. Case closed."

"I can't believe we're going to camp," Juni whispered to his sister. It had been a week since their parents had announced their plans at the ice-cream parlor. Ever since then, Mom had been enthusiastically labeling all their clothes with name tags.

Dad had stamped and addressed a dozen envelopes so Carmen and Juni could write snail mail letters home.

They'd outfitted the kids with bug spray, sun-block, sleeping bags, and clompy hiking boots.

And finally, early one July morning, they drove the kids to a parking lot to catch a bus.

A bus that would drive them to camp.

For three whole weeks.

After the Cortezes climbed out of the SUV, Dad grabbed Carmen and Juni in a fierce hug. "Oh, my babies are going to sleep-away camp!" he cried.

"Dad!" Carmen said in a muffled voice, her face squished into her dad's shoulder. "How come you didn't get this emotional when we went on that mission to the Sahara? That was sleep-away, too."

"Not to mention, superdangerous," Juni said morosely. "The most action we're gonna get at camp is catching fireflies in little jars."

"I guess we're just feeling a little nostalgic for camp ourselves," Mom explained, ruffling Juni's curls. "I went to horse camp when I was a girl. Ah, I still remember my trusty pony, Sasha."

"And I went to football camp in the Spanish countryside," Dad said. Being European, Dad called soccer football. "I made some of the best friends of my life at that camp."

His black eyes got wet and twinkly. Dad was prone to emotional outbursts.

"Avoid any mention of 'Kumbayah,'" Juni whispered to Carmen. "We don't want Dad to burst into tears!"

Just then, a strapping camp counselor in khaki shorts emerged from the bus. He hollered out into the parking lot, "All aboard, campers!"

"Oh, no," Carmen said. Suddenly, she was the one feeling a little weepy.

And Juni's bravado was melting away like bubble-gum ice cream on a sunny day.

As they'd pointed out, the Spy Kids had been on plenty of missions without their parents. They'd traveled to places all over the globe. But they'd had death-defying spy work to distract them. And besides, no mission had kept the family apart for three whole weeks.

"Well, this is it," Juni said, offering his cheek to Mom for one last kiss. Then he stood grimly before his father.

"Dad," he said.

"Junito," Dad said gruffly.

The male Cortezes threw themselves into each other's arms, sniffling loudly.

"Oh, brother," Carmen breathed, as she gave Mom a hug good-bye.

"'Oh, brother' is right, Carmenita," Dad said,

straightening up and wiping his eyes. "Remember, even if he is an international superspy, Juni is younger than you. You keep an eye out for him, okay, sweetheart?"

"And don't forget," Mom added, "you two are still partners, even if you will be staying in different cabins."

"Don't worry," Carmen said with a brusque nod. She didn't want to talk too much as she followed a line of campers onto the bus. In fact, the lump in her throat made talking sort of uncomfortable.

Juni seemed just as eager to change the subject. After he and Carmen had climbed onto the bus and found seats, he poked his head out the window. Mom and Dad were standing below them, their lips trembling.

"So, what are you guys going to do with yourselves while we're away?" Juni said.

"Oh, nothing much," Dad said, giving Mom a shifty glance.

"Maybe a little vacation in Tahiti," Mom added with a shrug. "A short cruise, perhaps."

"And don't forget the spa in Jamaica," Dad said.

"Oh," Juni said blankly. "Sounds great."

"We'll miss you terribly," Mom said quickly. "I'm sure we won't have nearly as much fun as you will."

Before the Spy Kids had a chance to reply, the bus began rolling out of the parking lot. All they could do was give their parents one last wave. And then, Carmen and Juni were on their way to—*ugh*—summer camp.

Hours later, the bus hit a big pothole and Juni awoke with a jolt. He slyly wiped a dribble of drool off his chin and peered out the window. He'd fallen asleep almost as soon as the bus had left the parking lot. He had no idea how long they'd been on the road. But he did know that the bus had taken them very far from home.

The bus turned onto a narrow dirt road and Juni could see a rough wooden sign.

He turned to Carmen, who was also conked out on the seat next to him.

"Hey!" he whispered, giving her a nudge. "I think we're here!"

Carmen opened one sleepy eye to glare at her brother.

"We'd better be," she growled, "or you're in big trouble for waking me up."

"Check it out," Juni said, pointing out the window. "I've gotta admit. It's kinda . . . nice."

Carmen peered out the window at the landscape—a lazy river, tons of trees and a smattering of rustic cabins. She nodded reluctantly.

"Very pretty," Carmen said. "But lots of lame things are pretty. Don't be deceived. What's that sign say?"

The bus was just about to pass beneath the archway. Juni peered at the rough lettering on the sign. Then he gasped.

"Oh my gosh!" he blurted. "Mom and Dad never told us what this camp is called."

"Yeah, so?" Carmen said. "Aren't all camps called Minnewonkatonka or Camp Kankakee or something like that?"

"Not this one!" Juni cried. "Look!"

Carmen gazed at the sign herself. Then she gasped too.

"'Camp Spy Valley—Owned and Operated by the Office of Strategic Services'?" she read. "Our parents were totally holding out on us. It's a camp for Spy Kids! "

As the bus rattled into the campgrounds, Carmen and Juni took a look at the other kids sitting around them.

"We should have *known* these were Spy Kids," Carmen whispered to her brother. "Check it out. They're all wearing spy watches."

Carmen and Juni were wearing spy watches, too. They never took them off. Not only did the big green-screened watch faces tell time, they also served as walkie-talkies, navigational systems, mini-computers, and villain trackers.

Plus they looked really cool.

The bus sputtered to a halt and all the Spy Kids began gathering their backpacks and giving one another shy smiles. But before they could start introducing themselves, a smiling man bounded up the bus steps. He was tall, with a big, jiggly belly and tree-stump legs clad in army green shorts. He wore a pumpkin-colored "Spy Valley" T-shirt that almost matched his wispy red hair, which was pulled back in a low ponytail. His beard was an even brighter shade of orange.

The man wore woven leather bracelets around each wrist and a string of Native American glass beads around his neck. He was beaming at the Spy Kids bustling around the bus aisle.

"Ah, my campers!" he announced. "Welcome to Spy Valley! Please report to the main lodge on the double. Time for orientation. And I'm not talking about some boring OSS briefing, either!"

The Spy Kids exchanged surprised glances. Everybody knew the OSS briefings were totally tedious. But few people came out and admitted it.

Raising his eyebrows at his sister, Juni hauled his backpack off the rack above their seat and tromped down the aisle. Then he jumped heavily down the bus steps, and crashed smack into a girl with pale-blond hair.

"Hey!" the girl squeaked. "Watch where you're . . . going . . ."

Before she could finish her sentence, the girl's blue eyes glazed over. She stared at Juni with her mouth hanging open.

Juni shifted uncomfortably and skimmed his finger beneath his nose. He hoped there wasn't something gross hanging out of it! Why else would this kid be staring at him like he was a fascinating science experiment?

"What's your name?" the girl asked.

"Uh, Juni," Juni blurted. "Juni Cortez. Sorry to crash into you like that."

"Oh," the girl said. "No problem. No problem at all. I'm Cecilia."

"Oh," Juni said, shuffling his feet. "So, are you new to the spy biz?"

"Completely," Cecilia said. "I'm Level Four. I was just recruited last month, right after my ninth birthday. My parents thought Spy Valley might help me polish some of my spy skills."

"Yeah, well, good luck with that," Juni said. He turned on his heel and headed toward the lodge. "See ya around."

"Or maybe *you* could help me polish my spy skills," Cecilia called after him.

"Huh?" Juni said, glancing back at her.

"You know, help me work my spy gadgets," Cecilia said shyly. "Or maybe do the obstacle course with me. Or we could just talk about spy stuff. Over dinner."

"Well, maybe . . . " Juni said hesitantly.

"Great!" Cecilia chirped. "So I'll see you soon?"

"Uh—"

"Okay!" the girl said with a grin. "See you, Juni!"

Then she skipped off to join a group of other nine-year-old girls. The girls all began staring at Juni and giggling behind their hands.

"Oooh," Carmen said, stealing up behind her brother. "Someone's got a big old crush on you!"

"What?" Juni sputtered. "She does not. Take it back!"

"Juni's got a girrrrl-frieeeeend!" Carmen taunted.

"Do! Not!" Juni shouted. He stomped away from his sister and toward the lodge. He could feel his cheeks burning.

Ew! Juni thought. I couldn't be less interested in Cecilia. First of all, she's only Level Four. That's like being in spy kindergarten! And second, she's a *girl.* And girls are so . . . girly. *Blech.*

I'll just have to avoid Cecilia at all costs, he thought as he ducked into the lodge. He quickly found a seat on a rough wooden bench. A seat between two scuff-kneed, tousle-haired *boys.* He let out a big sigh of relief.

Inside the lodge, Carmen watched Juni rush to sit between a couple of boys. She was on her own. She scanned the big wooden building. It was bustling with Spy Kids, from teenagers wearing fabulous gear to eight-year-olds who wouldn't know a rocket shoe from an auto-rappeller.

Spotting a row of girls who looked just about her age, Carmen made her way over to their bench and gave the group a wave.

"Hi, I'm Carmen," she said with a confident smile.

"Carmen Cortez?" said one girl with braces and shiny brown bangs. "Hi, I'm Beth. You're in our cabin! I saw your name on the list Spy Valley sent to our parents."

"Mom and Dad *really* held out on us," Carmen muttered with a little grin.

"Want to sit down?" said another girl sitting a few seats away from Beth. She flashed Carmen a glossy smile and flipped her hair over one of her tan shoulders. Carmen smiled back and sat down next to the girl.

"I'm Farrah," the girl introduced herself.

"And I'm Cheryl," said a girl sitting on Carmen's other side. She was just as glam as Farrah, with frosty white eye shadow and cornrows filled with glittery beads. "Welcome to Beta Cabin."

"Beta?" Carmen said, raising her eyebrows.

"Like the military," Cheryl said as she adjusted

her halter top. "All the SV cabins are named after Greek letters. We're Beta. Then there are the Alpha girls. They're fourteen—the oldest Spy Kids here. And the little girls are in Gamma. Over on the boys' side there's Delta, Epsilon, and Zeta."

"Delta," Farrah said with a long sigh. She fluttered her long mascara'd lashes. "That's the oldest boys' cabin. They're so-o-o-o cute."

Both Farrah and Cheryl were wearing platform flip-flops, belly-baring shirts, and lots of makeup. Farrah's blond hair was flipped into glossy wings around her face. She kept swooping the wings around as she peeked over her shoulder at the kids—the *boys*—sitting behind them.

Carmen peeked, too. The boys looked like they were fourteen. They had razor stubble and everything.

"Delta guys?" she whispered to Farrah.

"Tscha!" Farrah whispered back.

"Ahem!"

The man from the bus had taken the lodge stage and was looking out at the crowd of Spy Kids with a relaxed smile. Carmen and her cabin mates turned their attention forward.

"You made it," the man said. "A great test of any spy is the old, endless-bus-ride-to-camp torture."

Laughter rippled through the lodge.

"My name is Oscar Zohn," the man continued. "I'll be your camp director this evening, and in fact, all session long.

"And, as you also should be aware, any good spy knows who the boss is," Oscar continued. "So I'll save you the Web-hacking legwork and tell you about myself. I was a spy with the OSS for twenty-four years. You heard of the moon mission?"

"No way!" blurted one of the boys behind Carmen.

"'No way' is right," Oscar replied with a laugh. "I was nowhere near that mission! But I *was* on the team that averted the great water-balloon war of 'Ninety-eight."

"What water-balloon war?" one kid in the audience asked.

"Exactly!" Oscar said. "After I retired from active duty last year, the OSS asked me to create a summer camp for Spy Kids. After a lot of scheming and plotting, I think I've come up with quite a full three weeks for you. You're going to leave here much savvier spies than you are now. Even you Level Ones.

"At Camp Spy Valley," Oscar went on, "you're going to learn how to fight tougher and sneak around sneakier. You'll be taught how to convert ordinary hamburger, ketchup, and aluminum foil into a high-grade weapon. Or a delicious meal!"

"Now, we're talkin'," Juni said from his seat a few rows behind Carmen. Carmen cringed and turned around to glare at her brother. Could he think of *nothing* but snacking?

"You'll leave here the most cunning Spy Kids the world has ever seen," Oscar continued. "But you'll also, I hope, have lots of fun! Of course, there are a few rules. It wouldn't be an OSS camp without those, right?"

Carmen gave Farrah a knowing wink, and they both giggled.

"First rule: no snacks or sweets outside the mess hall."

"N-o-o-o-o-o-o!"

Carmen closed her eyes. Of course, that was her brother again. He was *so* embarrassing.

"Lights out at nine-thirty," Oscar continued. This elicited a groan from Farrah and Cheryl.

"I heard that," Oscar said with a wink. "But as we all know, the best spy work is done in the wee hours of the morning. So you need your rest. And just in case any Alphas or Deltas are tempted to sneak out of their cabins, know that there will be On-Duty counselors stationed around camp. And, this being an OSS camp, our OD counselors are robots. So they *never* fall asleep."

More groans filled the lodge. Then Oscar rubbed his hands together and said, "Now for the good stuff—the gadgets! Behind the mess hall, you will find the Gizmo Shed. It's stocked with hot-off-the-presses gadgetry, spy vehicles, and more. These are all at your disposal. Just be sure to fill in the sign-out sheet by the shed door."

Virtually every spy in the room began to murmur excitedly.

"Now, in your cabins," Oscar said finally, "you'll each find something waiting for you on your bunk. It's an up-to-the-minute, OSS-manufactured personal spy computer."

"Cool!" breathed some of the Deltas behind Carmen. She peeked over her shoulder at them. Then she did a double take.

Were the boys awestruck by the spy computers? Or were they talking about *her*? They were staring straight at her, and whispering to each other.

" . . . Cortez!" she heard one say.

" . . . famous spy," she caught from another Delta.

"*And* she's pretty!" said a third.

Carmen felt her face flush. She couldn't believe it. These Spy Kids had heard of her! And . . . they *liked* her!

Carmen shot a surprised glance at Farrah, who, of course, had been eavesdropping as well. She expected her cabin mate to nudge her with her elbow and collapse into another fit of giggles.

But instead, Farrah glared at Carmen with icy jealousy in her eyes.

In confusion, Carmen turned to Cheryl.

Her stare was even colder.

Taking male attention away from these sparkly spy girls, she realized, was a definite no-no.

This, Carmen thought, as she took in Cheryl's and Farrah's stony, pretty faces, could get very ugly.

CHAPTER 4

A gentle whirring filled the morning air the day after the Spy Kids' arrival at Camp Spy Valley. The sound wasn't the croak of bullfrogs waking up in the camp swimming hole. Or cicadas chirping in the bushes. Or a breeze rustling through lush summer greenery.

No, it was the sound of state-of-the-art plasma-screen video monitors unfurling out of tree trunks all over the campgrounds.

En masse, the screens flickered to life. A computer-generated image of steaming pancakes, orange juice, and brown-sugar-dotted oatmeal floated enticingly on every one.

Then a nasal, robotic voice rang out through the camp:

"Announcements, an-NOUNCE-ments, an-NOUNCE-ments! All campers, please report to the mess hall for breakfast. Be sure to watch your step!"

Juni walked with some of his Epsilon cabin

mates to the mess hall. At the door, they encountered a moving—make that, *whizzing*—sidewalk. As they peered into the dining room, they saw rustic chairs floating on super strong jets of air instead of legs.

"Man," said one strapping camper named Big John. "The OSS didn't miss a beat. This camp is completely wired."

"Yeah," said another kid named Toby. Toby was as short and wiry as Big John was big and burly. He shoved his glasses up on his nose. "I read that the OSS has planted close to half a million gigacircuits all over the grounds. There's an underground defense lair, a robotronic Loch Ness monster for creature-fighting practice, and *miles* of obstacle courses."

"Toby," Juni said with a sigh. "This is camp. Which means you don't have to do homework!"

"I like studying," Toby said. "It's one of the most important elements of spy work."

As he spoke, Toby stepped gingerly onto the speedy conveyer belt.

"Whoooooaaa!" he cried when the belt whisked him into the mess hall. He teetered back and forth as the moving sidewalk zipped him through the food line. A robotic arm shoved a tray into his hands and slapped a bowl of oatmeal onto it. Then the conveyer belt veered to the left.

"Whaaaaaaa!" Toby screamed. He fell face first into his oatmeal—only to be showered with a spray of orange juice at the beverage station.

By the time the conveyer belt dumped Toby at the end of the food line, he had a piece of cinnamon toast stuck to the back of his head and his glasses were clouded up with cold milk.

Juni shook his head as he stepped off the moving sidewalk behind Toby. His own tray was balanced securely in his hands and loaded with food.

"Level Fours," he muttered, rolling his eyes.

"Thinking about me?" said a sweet, slightly squeaky voice behind him. Juni jumped, then slowly, turned around.

"Oh," he said flatly. "Hi, Cecilia."

"So," Cecilia said, nibbling on a piece of toast, "where are you sitting, Juni?"

Juni racked his brains for all his best spy evasion tactics. He could use the Sproing Soles in his hiking boots to launch himself up to the ceiling. But then he'd have to drop his breakfast tray. Never!

He could chew on some of Uncle Machete's Cloud Cover gum. In 2.3 seconds, he'd be surrounded by an opaque purple cloud. It was a great camouflage, but, *hmmmm*, it lacked subtlety.

Then, out of the corner of his eye, Juni saw Toby stagger to his feet, digging oatmeal out of his ears.

"I'm . . . sitting with Toby here," Juni blurted, grabbing the skinny kid by the elbow. "I told him I'd share my breakfast with him after his little moving sidewalk disaster."

"You did?" Toby blurted.

"You did?" Cecilia whined.

Juni nodded emphatically. Then he saw an air-puffed chair float by. Thinking fast, he shoved Toby into the chair. Then he plopped into another chair floating right behind it.

"Enjoy that toast, Cecilia," Juni called over his shoulder as the chair whizzed to a table in a far corner. "See you around, maybe."

"Definitely!" the smitten Cecilia called after Juni.

As Juni sighed, Toby turned around in his floating chair. "Thanks for sharing your breakfast with me," he said, eyeing Juni's oatmeal hungrily. "My mom says that for a wiry kid, I can really pack it away."

Juni rolled his eyes.

"And thus begins my first full day at Camp Spy Valley," he said. "Just great."

—— * ——

"Announcements, an-NOUNCE-ments, an-NOUNCE-ments! Campers shall report to their spy training posts immediately after breakfast."

Carmen and her fellow Betas were clinging to the side of a cliff like long-legged bugs. Each girl wore a harness. And their harnesses were all connected to one another by a long, swagging rope.

In other words, if one Spy Kid went down, they all went down.

Even though a huge safety net was strung beneath the cliffside, Carmen and her other, ultra-competitive cabin mates were brutally afraid of a fall. Falling would mean they'd failed the team. And they'd brought shame on Beta Cabin. And they'd proved to be less-than-excellent spies.

Carmen, for one, would not let that happen.

She spotted a fingerhold three feet above her.

"Climbing," she shouted to her companions. Then, in one nimble movement, she jumped up the cliffside. She dug her fingers into the skinny crevice, then expertly found herself some tiny toeholds.

"Way to go, Cortez," Beth called from the base of the cliff.

But from Cheryl and Farrah, who'd climbed almost as high as Carmen, there was chilly silence.

Well, *almost* silence.

Suddenly, a buzzing sound emerged from the rear pocket of Cheryl's pink short-shorts.

Then a sparkly cloud flew out of the pocket.

And *then*, that swarm flew straight for Carmen!

"Ow!" Carmen squealed as she felt a little *zotz* on her neck. The spot immediately began stinging and itching.

More little metallic specks began landing all over her, stinging madly.

"Ow, ow, ow!" Carmen cried.

Finally, she could stand it no more. She released one of her fingerholds and slapped one of the specks on her upper arm. Barely clinging to the cliffside, she looked at her palm.

She was holding a tiny, crumpled, buggy thing with cellophane wings, wire legs, and a stinger the size of a small needle.

"Mechanical mosquitoes!" Carmen said. She shot Cheryl an evil look.

"Picked 'em up at the Gizmo Shed," Cheryl said. "They add an interesting wrinkle to spy training, don't you think?"

"They're *very* camp," Farrah said with a smirk. "Just like that wicked sunburn on your nose, Carmen. Ooh, that's gonna peel like crazy. You really should think about moisturizing."

With that, Farrah released her own handhold and pulled a small squirt gun from her utility belt.

"No spy," she said, "should be caught without . . . "

" . . . Precision-Aim Oil Slick," Cheryl finished. "You never know when you're going to need to get out of a tight spot."

"Oil?" Carmen squeaked.

"Slick," Farrah said. "As in the opposite of you, Carmen Cortez."

Farrah pulled the trigger.

"No!" Carmen cried as she watched a stream of oil fly through the air and land directly inside her precarious handhold. Her fingertips suddenly went slimy. Then she watched in horror as they began to slide out of their niche.

"Faaaaaaaallllllinnnnnggg!" Carmen cried as she plunged backward off the mountainside. One by one, her squealing cabin mates were yanked off the cliff with her.

"Tell us something we don't know," Farrah said as she landed in the safety net next to Carmen. She smirked as the other girls careened into the net and shot grumbling glances at Carmen.

"Okay, troops," the robot counselor announced

when the last girl had fallen. "That means we start climbing again. From the beginning."

As a collective groan rang out into the warm summer air, Carmen dusted off her hands and glowered at her new enemies.

"And thus begins my first full day at Camp Spy Valley," she muttered. "Just great."

"Announcements, an-NOUNCE-ments, an-NOUNCE-ments! All campers are required to e-mail your parents at least once a day."

That afternoon, Juni was walking back to Epsilon Cabin when he spotted Carmen. She was sitting on the front porch of Beta Cabin, typing on her Spy Valley laptop.

"Hey," Juni said glumly.

"What's wrong with you?" Carmen responded grumpily.

Juni held up a gleaming metal rod. As Carmen peered at it closely, she saw that it had all the knots and burls of a tree branch. But at its tip was a pulsing, glowing ember.

"I was just roasting up a hot dog with this self-flaming stick I found in the Gizmo Shed," Juni said. "And an OD robot found me out and confiscated it! And all my marshmallows, too!"

"Yeah," Carmen said. She'd spotted a couple of the OD robots on the campgrounds, too. They rolled around on all-terrain tires. They had surveillance cameras in their flashing red eyes and very strong robot claws. They were not to be messed with. "Life at Spy Valley is a bit rough."

"On the bright side," Juni said, "I learned how to make a rustic bomb-detection device in the macramé workshop. And I made Mom a cool pot holder!" He pulled a knitted object out of his pocket and showed it to Carmen.

Carmen eyed the macramé square with a raised eyebrow.

"Hmmm," she said, "don't I recall a certain someone saying that pot holders were totally *lame*?"

"It's every spy's prerogative to change his mind," Juni retorted. He still looked a little sheepish. Desperate for a subject change, he nodded at Carmen's laptop.

"Speaking of Mom," he said, "we might as well do our mandatory e-mail together."

Carmen nodded. With a few keystrokes, she logged into her Spy Valley e-mail system.

"You have one new message," said a robotic voice. Juni leaned over Carmen's shoulder to peer at their parents' message!

"Dear children, said the note. *We miss you so terribly. The beachside seafood dinner and calypso concert (with dancing!) we attended last night upon our arrival in Jamaica have been very little comfort. We are having . . . almost . . . no fun at all.*

But we are sure that you're having a ball at Camp Spy Valley. (Didn't we keep our little secret well?!) Hope you're enjoying all the training maneuvers, and there are some nice spies in your cabins. Write soon! Love and kisses, Mom and Dad."

"Well," Carmen said, "at least *some* Cortezes are having the time of their lives."

"Announcements, an-NOUNCE-ments, an-NOUNCE-ments! After dinner, gather around the campfire for a sing-along with your camp director, Oscar Zohn."

Juni was heading toward the clearing in front of the lodge. All the Spy Valley campers were congregating around a roaring campfire. And all eyes were trained on Oscar, who was strumming the first few chords of a droning folk song.

"Ugh," Juni muttered. "I wonder if our rock-and-roll-loving parents knew they were sending us to a camp where they played *folk* songs."

"Hi, Juni!"

Juni froze. Once again, Cecilia was lurking right behind him!

"Do you like this music?" Cecilia asked with a sweet smile. "You strike me as someone who'd be more into, hmmm, electric guitar."

"Well . . . " Juni said, blushing a little. Cecilia had him pegged. She saw how cool he was! But that still didn't make her less annoying!

"Hey, why don't we go for a walk in the woods," Cecilia continued. "I want to know all about Juni Cortez. Plus, it would be . . . romantic."

The *R*-word made Juni's blood run cold. He pulled at his T-shirt collar and began stammering out an elaborate and *long* excuse as to why he could not—under any circumstances—take a romantic walk through the woods with Cecilia.

At the bonfire, Carmen sat down on a fallen log and giggled as she watched Juni squirming under the attention of Cecilia.

"I wonder what she sees in my brother," Carmen muttered to herself. "Must be a Level Four thing."

Carmen glanced around her at the circle of campers. Everyone—except Carmen, that is—was gazing in rapture at Oscar Zohn.

"Jambalaya, m'lord, Jambalaya," Oscar was singing as he strummed his acoustic guitar. "Jambalaya, m'lord, Jambalaya . . . "

Ugh! Carmen thought. That folk music . . . it's awful! Why are all the other kids so into it?

Even cooler-than-thou Cheryl and Farrah had stopped fussing with their long, shiny hair and sparkly makeup. Their glossy mouths were hanging open and little tears were forming at the corners of their eyes.

Weird, Carmen thought.

As Oscar strummed some more, Carmen grinned slyly.

Lucky I have a little "defense," she thought. She reached into her shorts pocket and pulled out two tiny earplugs. She spun a dial on one of the ear-pieces to "rock and roll."

"Extra-mini Walkman," Carmen said to herself, sighing. "Sweet relief."

Setting the volume on HIGH, Carmen slipped the gadgets into her ears, secretly blocking out Oscar's voice and his guitar strummings. Then, for the first time all day, she relaxed.

And thus, she thought, as a loud, thumping drum solo flowed into her head, ends my first full day at Camp Spy Valley. Oh, brother!

CHAPTER 5

In the mess hall the next day, Carmen stepped onto the moving sidewalk and whizzed through the lunch line. She grabbed a tuna sandwich and held up her glass so a robotic spout could fill it with grape bug juice. That was the Spy Valley name for Kool-Aid. As Farrah would have said, it was *very* camp. And, as an added bonus—drinking bug juice turned your mouth a funky shade of purple, pink, or green, depending on the flavor.

After she'd filled her tray, Carmen hopped onto one of the floating chairs and giggled as it bobbed her lightly through the dining room.

Carmen's second morning at Spy Valley had been much better than the first. She and her cabin mate, Beth, had teamed up for a jet-kayak relay race. And they'd totally beaten Cheryl and Farrah!

The thought of the victory brought another grin to Carmen's face. In fact, she was so immersed in daydreaming about her big triumph, she paid no attention to where her floating chair was floating to—until it plopped her at an almost full table. Carmen looked around and gasped. Sitting at the table was her annoying brother, a sulky Cheryl and Farrah, and that nerdy kid, Toby. Before Carmen could even say hello, the last seat at the table was filled by Juni's new girlfriend, Cecilia.

"Hiiiii, Juuuuni," Cecilia sighed as she put down her tray.

"Save me," Juni whispered, looking up at the ceiling.

"Campers!" Oscar Zohn's voice boomed from the back of the mess hall. "Eyeballs up front, please. I have an announcement."

"Thanks!" Juni whispered to the ceiling with a grin. He turned with the rest of the campers to look at Oscar.

"Spy Kids," he said, "it's that moment you've all been waiting for. Mission time!"

Immediately, the room filled with a loud clattering. The Spy Kids jumped out of their chairs. Many of them reached into their camp-issued canvas spy bags and pulled out gadget-laden vests and utility belts. They snapped on their gear and synchronized their spy watches. Then they stuffed their pockets with bread and butter for lunch on the run.

Finally, en masse, they dropped into kung fu fighting stances.

They were ready to save the world!

"Uh, heh-heh," Oscar said nervously. "Um . . . at ease, troops. I meant a *mock* mission."

"Oh," said many of the Spy Kids. Laughing along with Oscar Zohn, they took their seats again. Only Carmen and Juni looked megadisappointed.

"Let me explain," Oscar said. "You've all heard about the 'color wars' that they have at other camps, right?"

"Sure," Toby piped up, jumping to his feet. "The camp divides up into teams and the campers compete in games. The color war teaches campers leadership, ingenuity, and team-building skills."

Toby pushed his glasses farther up his nose and sat down. Juni rolled his eyes.

"Good studying, Toby!" Oscar said cheerily. "Well, here at Spy Valley, we do things a little differently. We have . . . a Spy War!"

"Coooool," breathed the Spy Kids at once.

"Here's the dealio, kids," said Oscar eagerly. "I have hidden a secret 'treasure' somewhere on the grounds of Camp Spy Valley."

"That's five hundred acres," Toby gasped.

"Uh-huh," Oscar said. "Five hundred acres of

some of the most diverse terrain in the country. We've got it all here at Spy Valley—marshy swampland, dense forest, a desert, bubbling tar pits, sunny ponds and lakes, underwater caves. . . . "

"So what's the treasure?" called out one of the Epsilon boys.

"Oh, if I told you, it wouldn't be a secret, would it?" Oscar said. His forehead started to look a little shiny and his eyes shifted back and forth. He appeared almost nervous. "And besides, the treasure is inconsequential. A mere trinket I use for the purpose of the mission.

"Of course, the real object of the Spy War is the hunt!" Oscar said.

"I've rigged Spy Valley's grounds with all sorts of crazy roadblocks and challenges," Oscar continued with another grin. "It is your job to outwit these obstacles and track down that treasure. The winning team will receive a pennant, all the ice cream they can eat, and a special commendation to the OSS.

The idea of such glory sent a thrill up Carmen's spine. She just *had* to win the Spy War. That would show Cheryl and Farrah!

Carmen glanced at Juni, who was sitting next to her at the table.

"Don't forget," Mom had said to them before they'd come to camp, "you're still partners, even if you will be staying in separate cabins."

It was true. Carmen and Juni had learned long ago that they did their best spy work as spy partners. It went without saying that they would be on the same team.

But who else should they recruit?

Carmen locked eyes with Beth, who was sitting a few tables away.

"Teammates?" Carmen mouthed at her new friend.

"Totally," Beth whispered back. She flashed Carmen a smile and a thumbs-up.

Carmen turned to Juni.

"I've got Beth on our team," she whispered. "We are *so* going to win this thing."

"I've got a few Epsilon kids in mind," Juni whispered back to her. "They're strong, smart, completely with it. I'll see if I can get them to sign on to our team."

"Okay," Carmen said. "We're in bus—"

"I bet you're wondering who will be on your teams," Oscar said. "Well, that's simple. Just look around your lunch tables."

"Uh-oh," Juni whispered.

Carmen felt her heart sink.

"Is he saying what I think he's saying?" she asked her brother.

"Your lunch buddies," Oscar continued, "are now your teammates. Each table of six campers will become a company in the Spy War army."

Carmen and Juni gazed around the table.

Cheryl was glaring at Carmen with sullen, brown eyes.

Farrah would have been sneering at Carmen, too, if she hadn't been too busy applying her post-lunch lip gloss.

Swoony Cecilia was gazing at Juni with a look of rapture on her face.

And Toby was already busy unfolding a detailed topographical map of the Spy Valley acreage. Of course, as he jotted notes in the map's margins, he spilled his milk in Carmen's lap.

"*This* is our team?" Carmen whispered to Juni as she mopped up her milk-soaked shorts.

"This is our team," Juni groaned. "Looks like we've got our work cut out for us."

CHAPTER 6

The next morning, Carmen and her teammates met on a remote grassy hill behind the Spy Kids' cabins. After making sure no other teams were nearby, the six kids formed a circle on the ground. Carmen planted her fists on her knees and regarded the motley crew. Farrah and Cheryl, as usual, were busy primping. Cecilia was staring adoringly at Juni. Toby's nose was buried in a spy manual. And Juni seemed preoccupied with a large, flat, burlap-covered object sitting on the grass next to him.

Carmen heaved a big sigh. Then she began to speak.

"Okay, spies," Carmen said. "We've had approximately twelve hours to hatch some plans. Let's compare notes. Farrah, what did you come up with?"

Farrah sneered at Carmen. But when she glanced at Cheryl, her 'tude melted away. In fact, she collapsed into a fit of giggles.

"You tell them, Cheryl," Farrah squealed.

"No, you!" Cheryl cried.

"No, you!"

"No—"

"Um," Juni blurted, "how about you both tell us!"

"Well, duh, Juni!" Cecilia said, batting her eyelashes at him.

"Ugh," Juni muttered.

"Okay, okay, okay," Farrah said. She gave her hair an extra-bouncy flip. "Yesterday, Cheryl and I did what Spy Kids do best. We spied, of course!"

"On?" Carmen asked.

"Team number six, otherwise known as the Powers," Cheryl volunteered.

"Isn't that the team made up almost entirely of Delta boys?" Carmen said slyly.

"Yeah!" Farrah said defensively. "What of it, Cortez?"

"Nothing," Carmen said, rolling her eyes. "So what did you find out?"

"Well, the Deltas—er, the Powers—are going to be tracking the treasure on the far eastern side of the Spy Valley property," Farrah said. "Over near the bubbling tar pits. So I think that's an excellent place to start."

"Uh-huh," Carmen said dryly. Then she turned to Cecilia. "What did you come up with, Cecilia?"

"Um, I didn't know we were supposed to do homework before the mission," Cecilia said, her cheeks going bright pink. "Is that the way it's usually done?"

"Yeah," Carmen said gently. "That's the way it's usually done."

"Quit picking on her," Cheryl said, putting a pseudo protective arm around Cecilia's shoulders. "After all, Toby and Juni didn't do any prep work, either. I happen to know they spent all of yesterday afternoon just puttering around the arts-and-crafts cabin. Maybe they're more interested in making pot holders for Mommy than winning the Spy War."

Juni shook his head and said nothing. He simply reached for the object sitting on the grass next to him. With a dramatic flourish, he whipped its burlap cover away. The entire team gasped.

"Puttering, eh?" Juni snickered. "I guess you *could* call it that. I call it converting Toby's topographical map into a highly detailed, pottery scale model of Camp Spy Valley."

"Ooooh," the teammates breathed together.

The clay sculpture was enormous and beautifully glazed. And it seemed no corner of Spy Valley's oddly treacherous landscape—from the super-sucking whirlpool to the spiky cactus patch to the bubbling tar pits—had been overlooked.

"What do those lights mean?" Cecilia asked. She pointed at several red lightbulbs flashing on the scale model.

"I'll defer to my partner on that one," Juni said. "Toby?"

"Thank you, Juni," Toby said briskly. With a flick of his skinny wrist, he unfurled a long pointer.

"Using a complex geotrigonometric formula and a voice analysis of Oscar Zohn's mission objective, I've calculated the ten most likely locations for the hidden treasure," Toby said. "As you can see from the flashing red lights, these locations are scattered far and wide across the campgrounds."

"Good work, guys," Carmen said.

"Not good enough!" Farrah cut in. "Why are there no red lights by the tar pits? The Powers are going there. They must know something!"

"But we know more," Juni said simply. "So I guess the question is, do we want to win the Spy War? Or do we want to make goo-goo eyes at the Deltas?"

Both Cheryl and Farrah bit their lips in anguish. Finally, their competitive spirit won out.

"Whatever," Farrah said in irritation. "We'll go check out your silly little flashing lights."

"But which one should we hit first?" Cheryl asked.

"The underwater cave, of course," Carmen said. She pointed at a murky blue section of Juni's scale model.

"Oh really?" Farrah pouted. "Now you're the most popular girl at Spy Valley *and* the smartest?"

Carmen sighed another deep sigh. Then she pulled her laptop out of her canvas spy bag. Quickly booting up, she did a speedy search of the OSS's top-secret intelligence files. Then she showed her laptop screen to Farrah and Cheryl with an exaggerated yawn.

"Eighty-six percent of all buried treasure has been found in underwater caves," Cheryl read aloud sullenly. "Okay . . . fine! The cave it is."

The Spy Kids pulled themselves to their feet and looped their gear-stuffed spy bags over their shoulders.

"Wait! Before we go, we have one more important thing to discuss," Juni piped up. "We've got to come up with a team name."

"Yeah!" Farrah gushed, jumping up and down. "I've got a fabulous one. Oscar's Angels."

"Um, hasn't that been done already?" Carmen asked.

"Okay, negativo," Farrah challenged. "Come up with a better name, then."

Carmen frowned in thought. As she tried to come up with a title for their ragtag team, she glanced at her brother. Then suddenly, the perfect name occurred to her.

"I've got it!" she said.

"No, *I've* got it," Juni cried.

Then Carmen and Juni spoke together: *"El Mejor!"*

As the Spy sibs looked at each other in surprise, Cecilia piped up, "Um, I guess speaking Spanish is another spy skill I haven't mastered yet. Translation, please?"

"*El Mejor,*" Carmen said. "It means 'the best'!"

The team paused. Then, one by one, each Spy Kid flashed a thumbs-up. Even Cheryl and Farrah.

"All right, *El Mejor,*" Juni cried, jumping to his feet with the rest of the kids. "To the underwater cave!"

"This is disgusting," Cheryl complained a couple hours later. "Remind me, whose idea was it to go to this stupid underwater cave?"

After stopping at the Gizmo Shed for more supplies, *El Mejor* had hiked straight to the site of the cavern. Now they were wading waist-deep through the dankest, smelliest, darkest water they'd ever seen. Even with their thick rubber diving suits and halogen headlamps, the cave was still cold, scary, and very, very gross.

What's more, they hadn't seen a glimmer of hidden treasure since they'd arrived.

To make matters worse, the water was getting murkier.

And deeper.

And smellier.

When the swirling water reached Cecilia's chin, the group stopped moving.

"I think it's time for our jellyfish," Carmen said.

Each Spy Kid reached into his or her waterproof gear bag, and pulled out a small rubber bundle. Unfurled, the bundles became floppy rubber suits. The Spy Kids stepped into the suits and zipped them from head to toe. They fitted plastic masks over their faces. Finally, they tugged on rip cords dangling from the front of each suit.

Shoop! Shoop! Shoop! Shoop! Shoop! Shoop!

Instantly, the suits inflated into big, squishy, transparent blobs equipped with several robotic arms. One arm had a claw on its tip. Another had a shovel. And yet another sported a beeping metal detector. Inside the suits were computer control panels, two-way radios, and a joystick. There were even watertight sleeves that the kids could poke their hands through if they needed to pick something up with their fingers.

With a bubbling *blurp*, the oxygen-filled jellyfish suits sank beneath the murky water.

Juni giggled with delight as his suit descended gracefully into the cavern. He moved his joystick forward and his suit began undulating gently through the water.

"*Just* like a jellyfish!" he exclaimed. His voice echoed through the speakers in each of the jellyfish suits.

"Check this out," Toby said, manipulating his control panel. Juni saw one of Toby's translucent robotic arms reach out and scoop some silt off the cave floor.

"Spying is *SO* fun!" Cecilia cried as she whooshed past Juni in her blobby suit.

Even Cheryl and Farrah were enjoying the suits so much that they stopped complaining about their ruined hair and makeup.

"We are so going to find the treasure with these

things," Carmen said.

"Except . . . " Juni said.

"Except *what*?" blurted the rest of the Spy Kids.

"Except our search just got three times harder," Juni answered. He pointed up ahead with one of his jellyfish arms. When the kids peered through the murky water, they saw that their big underwater cave had just divided into three separate caverns.

"Oh, man!" Toby said. "This is going to take all day!"

"Not if we split up," Carmen proposed. "We can divide into pairs. Each pair will search one of the caves. It'll be safe as long as we stay in radio contact."

"Great!" Cecilia said. Her jellyfish suit bobbed up and down excitedly. "Juni and I can take the cave on the left!"

"No!" Juni shouted.

"Hey," Cecilia whimpered, sounding hurt.

"I mean," Juni stammered, "you know, Carmen and I are partners. We usually do this kind of thing together."

Carmen just giggled. But when Juni shot her a desperate look, she threw her brother a bone.

"Sorry, but Juni's right, Cecilia," she said into her speaker. "You can't break up the Cortezes. So

Juni and I will search the left cavern. Farrah and Cheryl, you can take the middle one. And Toby and Cecilia—you guys can search the last cave."

"All right," Cecilia muttered. She turned around and undulated into the right cavern.

"Wait for meeeeee!" Toby cried, bouncing after her in his blobby suit.

As Farrah and Cheryl swam into the center cavern, Carmen and Juni delved into the one on the left. For a while, the Spy Kids bobbed along in silence. They sifted through mud with their robotic arms, shone their headlamps along the craggy ceiling, and investigated nooks and crannies with their extendable periscopes.

But after another hour of searching yielded no treasure, the Spy Kids were ready to throw in the towel.

"Let's hit my scale model again," said Juni sighing into his radio speaker. "This is a total bust—"

"Treasure!"

Farrah's thrilled voice echoed through the jellyfish speakers.

"Huh?" all the Spy Kids cried.

"Come quick!" Farrah screamed. "I totally tracked the treasure down!"

CHAPTER 7

Carmen spun her gelatinous jellyfish suit around and headed out of the cavern with Juni in tow. As she undulated into Farrah and Cheryl's cave, she couldn't help but feel a jealous pang.

I can't believe Farrah found the treasure, she thought. *I was sure she'd be too busy fixing her eye shadow to do any real spying!*

Then Carmen shook her floaty jellyfish head and scolded herself: *you have to be a team player,* she thought. *And if Farrah's won the Spy War for* El Major, *well, that's a good thing. Isn't it?*

Carmen didn't have any more time to wrestle with her conscience. She and Juni had come upon Cheryl and Farrah. They were hovering just inside their cavern entrance, looking at one of the slimy walls. When Carmen floated up to Farrah's side, Farrah huffed in exasperation.

"Bummer!" she sighed. "It was right here—a sparkly pot of jewels. I was just about to grab it when something sucked it back into this hole in the wall. Then this little door closed in front of it."

The Cortez kids looked at the wall. There was indeed a little door wedged into it. It was metal decorated with an ornate scrolly design.

Juni used his jellyfish arms to prod at the door. It didn't budge. Then he felt around the door's edges with his fingertips. It was positively sealed.

Finally, Juni fiddled with a rocky, round bump in the center of the little door. He was surprised when the bump turned. It was a dial.

Which meant that this was the door to a safe.

"Ladies," Juni announced. "This is your lucky day. Because Carmen Cortez happens to be the best safecracker in the OSS. Have at it, sis."

Juni floated out of the way. Carmen shot Farrah and Cheryl a nervous glance as she undulated up to the safe for closer examination. As she spun the dial, she heard a faint click in her jellyfish speaker and cringed. This was going to be one tough safe to crack. If she couldn't do it, Farrah and Cheryl would totally mock her.

On the other hand, she thought, if I *can* do it, they'll think I'm a stuck-up superspy. Basically, I can't win.

Carmen felt her shoulders slump for an instant.

But then she shook her head again.

What are you, she asked herself—a spy or a jellyfish? This is about completing a mission and winning the Spy War. Not impressing these totally mean and silly girls.

Carmen squinted at the dial. She typed a few commands into her control panel and a stethoscope floated out of her jellyfish suit. She pressed the stethoscope to the safe door. Then she began spinning the dial and listening to the subtle clicks and whirs that are every safecracker's guideposts.

Squinting hard, Carmen spun the dial to the left. Then a smidge to the right. And finally, she spun the dial left and yanked on the safe door with all her might. With a burst of air bubbles and a huge creaking noise, the door swung open.

"Yes!" Juni cried.

"You rock!" Cheryl said.

Despite herself, Carmen felt her cheeks flush with happiness.

"Grab the treasure!" Farrah cried.

Carmen grinned and reached deep into the dark niche in the wall. She felt around for a pot of jewels. But the safe seemed to be empty.

Carmen reached in further. And then, she felt something.

But it didn't feel like jewels.

In fact, it felt cold.

And slimy.

And *disgusting*!

With a terrified squeal, Carmen pulled her hand out of the safe. Tangled up in her fingers were glistening, purple fish guts!

"Gross!" Carmen screamed, flailing her hand wildly. Gruesome fish innards floated everywhere.

"What a weird treasure!" Juni said.

"That's *no* treasure," Carmen snapped. She glared at Cheryl and Farrah.

Their jellyfish suits were bobbling and jiggling extra hard. Inside them, the vindictive Spy Girls were howling with laughter.

"Guess your spy skills aren't so brilliant, after all," Farrah cried.

"That's it!" Carmen shouted. She began undulating angrily toward the giggling girls. "I've *so* had it with your pranks. We're going to settle this, and we're going to settle this now—"

"Aaaaaaigggh!"

A piercing scream echoed out of their speakers.

"Get 'em off me!" Cecilia cried.

"Help!" Toby shrieked.

"They're in trouble!" Juni cried.

"We've got to find them!" Carmen yelled. Forgetting about the fish guts and Farrah and Cheryl, she began typing wildly on her control panel. Finally, she found the command she was looking for—turbo speed.

With the other Spy Kids close on her heels, Carmen zoomed out of the cavern. In only a few seconds, they'd swum into Cecilia and Toby's cave.

As they undulated through the murky water, Juni cried out, "I think I see them!"

Carmen squinted through the gloom.

"Oh, yeah!" she agreed. "I see them, too. Blobby suits, twelve o'clock."

As Carmen gunned her jellyfish suit toward Cecilia and Toby, she gasped.

"Um, Cheryl and Farrah, what's your location?" she quavered into her speaker.

"Duh, we're right behind you, fish breath," Cheryl said.

Carmen didn't even bother to retort to the name-calling.

"Okay, if you're not up ahead with Cecilia and Toby," she said, "then what are . . . those?!"

Juni gasped.

"You're right," he breathed. "There're *four* blobs!"

"Help!" Toby and Cecilia shrieked.

Finally, the Spy Kids reached their teammates.

Or at least, Cecilia.

She was still screaming.

And her jellyfish suit was surrounded by three human-size, brown, shapeless creatures!

"Ew!" Farrah shrieked, pointing at the blobs with one of her robotic arms. "What are those *things* all over Cecilia?"

Juni held his breath and squinted at the gruesome predators. They were slimy and mushy and mud-colored. They didn't seem to have any limbs—just tiny black eyes and very, very big mouths.

Big, suckering mouths with lots of little teeth.

"They're . . . " Juni gasped, "they're giant—"

"Leeches!" Toby cried.

Juni heard Toby's voice but he couldn't see Toby's jellyfish suit. He spun around, scanning the murky cavern wildly.

"Over here!" Toby shrieked. Finally, Juni spotted him. Toby's suit was lying on its side on the floor. All its robotic arms had been ripped off. Juni sped over to his fallen fellow spy and nudged him into a sitting position.

"I . . . I tried to fight them off," Toby cried. His glasses were askew on his nose and he was staring at

Juni with watery eyes. "But they were too strong."

"That's okay," Juni told him. "It's four to three, now. We'll sock it to those slimeballs in no time."

Quickly, he swam back to Carmen, Farrah, and Cheryl.

"Okay," he said. "Let's surround them and beat 'em off."

Farrah, Cheryl, Carmen, and Juni formed a circle around the leeches, which were yanking and pulling at Cecilia's jellyfish suit while the little Level Four screamed in terror.

Farrah gave Carmen a challenging sneer, then bonked one of the leeches on the head with her robotic arm.

"Ha!" she cried as the leech turned toward her, its suckering mouth opening in surprise. "That got your attention!"

The leech responded by spitting a huge gob of slime right onto Farrah's face mask. Some of the slime spattered onto Cheryl's jellyfish suit, too.

"Gross!" the Spy Girls shrieked.

"I'm so outta here," Cheryl screamed.

"Wait for me!" Farrah squealed.

Before Carmen and Juni could say a word, the squeamish Spy Girls had undulated themselves right out of the cave.

The Cortez kids were on their own.

"Help meeeeee!" Cecilia continued to shriek. Then she screamed in terror as a leech ripped off one of her suit's robotic arms. It sucked the arm into its mouth, chewing on it mushily.

"That does it," Carmen said.

She thought about Farrah and Cheryl's snotty pranks.

She thought about Oscar Zohn's impossible Spy War.

She thought about mechanical mosquitoes and fish guts and floating mess-hall chairs.

And then, she channeled all of those thoughts into . . . her right foot.

"Hiiiiii-YAH!" Carmen shouted as she spun in a neat circle, then flared her foot through the water. She caught the leech with a roundhouse kick—right in its masticating sucker mouth.

"Take that!" Carmen shouted. She watched in satisfaction as the robotic arm shot out of the leech's mouth.

"Yes!" Carmen cried. She flashed Juni a thumbs-up. But to her surprise, his face was contorted with horror.

"What?" Carmen said. Then she looked to her right.

"Aaaaah!" she screamed.

When Carmen had knocked the jellyfish arm out of the leech's mouth, she'd plunged her foot right *into* its mouth. And now, the leech was chewing on *her.*

"Juni!" cried Carmen and Cecilia at once.

Juni gaped at his floundering fellow spies. Then he grabbed blindly at one of the leeches.

"Get . . . off . . . them," he grunted. But the giant worm was too slimy. Juni slid right off it. In desperation, he scanned his jellyfish-suit control panel.

"Silt sifter," he read, "periscope, halogen lamp, magnifying glass. This suit is good for nothing but research."

"Um, speaking of research . . . " said a voice in Juni's ear. It was Toby. Juni spun around and glanced at the Level Four spy. He was still sitting on the cave floor, but now he was typing away at his control panel.

"I've booted up my suit's info-puter," Toby said. "And I think I've found something."

"No time for that now," Juni huffed, turning away from Toby and taking another ineffectual swipe at one of the giant leeches. "This fight doesn't need brains. It needs brawn."

"Tell me about it," Carmen cried. The leech that

was making a chew toy of her leg was making its way up to her knee! "Do something, Juni!"

"Fire!" Toby cried.

"What?" Juni said between punches. "We're Spy Kids, Toby. We don't use guns. Even a Level Four should know that."

"Duh," Toby retorted. "But do you have a match? Leeches are deathly afraid of any kind of fire or heat. They like it cold and slimy."

Wait a minute! Juni thought suddenly.

His self-flaming stick was still stashed in his spy bag!

Pulling one hand back inside his jellyfish suit, he grabbed the retracted metal stick. Then he thrust it out into the water and pressed a button. Immediately, the gadget extended into a long, knobby metal rod.

Juni held his breath and pressed another button.

It worked! Despite being submerged in water, the end of the stick suddenly burst into life. Its end glowed orange and hot.

Juni merely had to wave the self-flaming stick at Carmen's leech and it opened its sucker mouth to let out a howl of fear.

Carmen pulled her foot out of the worm's mouth and swam out of the way.

"Thanks, Juni!" she cried.

"No prob," Juni said. Then he waved his stick at leech number two, which was trying to smush Cecilia's jellyfish suit against the cave wall.

This leech, too, let out a shriek of terror and retreated into the cave's shadows.

The last, stubborn leech held onto Cecilia. No matter how much Juni brandished the self-flaming stick, the leech simply darted out of the way. And it wouldn't let go of the Spy Girl.

"It's not working!" Juni cried to Carmen and Toby. "What now?"

"I don't know," Toby shrieked. "The info-puter says fire is our best weapon against leeches."

Carmen swam up next to Juni and began pummeling the leech with her fists. But the giant worm didn't even flinch.

"Man," Carmen muttered as she bounced off the creature. "This is enough to make me forget about finding that stupid treasure altogether!"

The minute the words left her mouth, the leech unlatched its sucker mouth from Cecilia's jellyfish suit. Still shrieking, the Spy Girl floated away. Then the leech simply swam into another shadowy corner of the cavern.

"Huh?" Juni said. "What just happened?"

Carmen spun around in confusion. All the leeches seemed to have disappeared entirely.

"I don't know," she said, grabbing Cecilia's jellyfish suit by the collar. "But I do know one thing. You should never look a gift leech in the mouth. Grab Toby and let's get outta here!"

"*Definitely* no prob," Juni said, speeding over to the fallen Spy Boy and scooping him up with one of his robotic arms. "Over and out!"

CHAPTER 8

Back at camp, it took Carmen a full half hour of scrubbing to get rid of the muddy, stinky grime from the underwater cavern.

As she emerged from her cabin, she heard the now familiar hum of plasma screens descending out of tree trunks.

"Announcements, an-NOUNCE-ments, an-NOUNCE-ments! All campers will be rewarded for their hard day of treasure-hunting with a campfire sing-along!"

Great, Carmen thought dryly. As she trudged toward the campfire, she recalled the e-mail she'd gotten from her parents after arriving home from the failed mission:

Dear Carmen and Juni,

Greetings from Costa Rica! You know the drill—we'd just begun our vacation when the OSS called with a mission! A thief had made off with a thermonuclear Earth-

shaker and hidden it somewhere on this island. And you know *how pesky thermonuclear Earth-shakers can be if you lose track of them!*

Luckily, we had one of Uncle Machete's gadgets handy. He calls it a Jitterbug. It can detect even the slightest underground tremor. We found the "buried treasure" in a record three hours. Then we decided we liked Costa Rica so much, we'd just continue our vacation here!

So how's Spy Camp? Tell us about all the fun things you're doing! We miss you terribly. And really, without you here, we're barely having any fun at all.

All our love, Mom and Dad

Carmen sighed. If only her mission could be that simple. But this Spy War was kicking her butt. As she slumped onto a log in the campfire clearing, she glanced at the other Spy Kids sitting around her. They looked as weary as she felt. They were covered with bruises, scratches, and discouraged scowls.

One of them, in particular, was sporting some seriously bad hair. His red curls were matted and sproinging in every direction.

"Hey," Juni said to his sister as he tried to run his fingers through the crazed curls. Halfway through, his fingers got caught in a vicious tangle. So Juni shrugged and gave up. He plopped down on the log next to Carmen.

"That's one cool thing about being away from the 'rents," Juni admitted. "Nobody's telling me to comb my hair!"

"You're gross," Carmen teased. But then she got serious. "You know, if Mom and Dad *were* here, maybe we'd have won the Spy War by now. Did you get that e-mail about their mission in Costa Rica?"

"Yeah," Juni sighed. "Do you think we've lost our touch?"

"Either that," Carmen said slowly, "or . . . "

She stopped talking when she saw Oscar Zohn enter the campfire circle. He gave the campers a jovial wave, pulled his guitar out of his case, and began strumming a drippy tune.

"I gave my love a bank," he sang, "that had no loan. . . . "

"Or what?" Juni whispered to Carmen. He winced as the dorky folk song filled the air.

Carmen looked around at their fellow Spy Kids. All gossiping, laughing, or groaning about Spy War wounds had utterly ceased. They were listening to the yucky folk music with completely rapt attention.

"Or . . . I don't know yet," Carmen said. *Something* just didn't feel right about this whole Spy Valley vibe. But she couldn't put her finger on what that something was. "Besides, I can't think straight with this folk music in my head."

"I know," Juni said, curling his lip.

"I have an antidote," Carmen whispered with a sly grin. She reached into her pocket and pulled out four tiny earpieces. She handed two of them to Juni.

"Mini-Walkman," she whispered. "Just plug 'em in and groove to the alterna-tunes."

"Cool," Juni said. He shoved the earplugs into his ears and sighed with happiness as heavy guitar sounds filled his head. "At least the day's ending better than it began."

"Just wait," Carmen whispered ruefully. "Tomorrow morning, it's back to the treasure hunt." Then she sighed and cranked up the volume on her own Walkman.

The next morning, *El Mejor* gathered again on their grassy hill. They were staring sullenly at Juni's scale model.

"Back to the treasure hunt," Cecilia moaned. "I vote we go somewhere dry today."

"Tscha," Farrah said. "I heard that the Powers almost got sucked into an extra-sticky tar pit yesterday."

"No!" Cheryl cried.

"Don't worry," Farrah said dramatically, placing a hand over her heart. "All the Deltas are safe."

"Whew," Cheryl breathed.

"Whatever," Carmen and Juni muttered.

"What else did you hear?" Toby asked Farrah. He pulled a notebook and pen from his pocket and got ready to take notes.

"Well, I heard one team got caught in a nest of snapping poison oak," Farrah said.

"*Snapping* poison oak?" Juni asked. "As in biting?"

"Uh-huh," Farrah said. "They're all in the infirmary with little tooth marks in their ankles."

"Well, I heard something, too," Cecilia said. "Something about vicious nibbling tadpoles. A team wanted to search a stream on the western border of the campgrounds. But the tadpoles wouldn't let them get anywhere near it."

Juni pulled a tangle of plastic strings out of his pocket. He frowned as he began weaving the strings into a pretty purple-and-yellow lanyard. When he noticed the other Spy Kids staring at him, he sputtered, "What? Arts and crafts helps me think!"

"And what are you thinking?" Cecilia asked, smiling sweetly at Juni.

Juni paused in his weaving.

"I'm thinking . . . " he said slowly, "doesn't this

'mission' seem a little weird to you? I mean, this is supposed to be a *mock* Spy War. For, like, training and fun. But what's fun about getting your ankles bitten by poison oak?"

"Or almost getting smooshed to death by giant leeches?" Carmen chimed in. Clearly, Juni had been nagged by the same doubts she was having. Something fishy was going on at Camp Spy Valley.

"Does it seem like Oscar's making this treasure hunt a bit too dangerous?" Juni went on. "I mean, even for international superspies?"

Carmen nodded. She and Juni looked expectantly at their *El Mejor* teammates.

They weren't nodding.

They were staring blankly at the Cortez kids. But then, at exactly the same moment, their expressionless faces turned scowly. They all began yammering angrily.

"Don't say mean things about Oscar," Toby said. "He's brilliant!"

"And s-o-o-o-o-o sweet," Farrah said. "He only wants the best for us. You guys are supercynical, even for spies."

"What?" Juni said. He gazed at his teammates in confusion. Finally, he looked to Cecilia. Surely, *she* would agree with him.

Strangely, Cecilia seemed to forget her crush on Juni as soon as he turned on their camp director.

"Oscar's the greatest," she declared. "How could anyone who makes such beautiful music be bad?"

"Juni's not saying Oscar's *bad*," Carmen said, jumping into the fray. "Just . . . maybe . . . a little nuts?"

"Nuts?!" cried Toby, Cecilia, Farrah, and Cheryl en masse.

Okay, Carmen thought. Perhaps I hit a nerve with that one!

"Listen, if you Cortezes feel that way, maybe you don't belong in *El Mejor*," Cheryl said poutily.

"Yeah, we do," Carmen said adamantly. No way was Cheryl kicking them off their own team!

"Fine," Cheryl said. "Then you won't mind going with us to search the cactus patch today."

"The cactus patch?" Juni squeaked. "The one with the shooting cactus spikes?"

"What?" Carmen blurted.

"I heard about it at breakfast," Juni said. "Yesterday, one of the teams came back from there with all sorts of unplanned piercings."

"Ow," Carmen said.

"Hey, if we can find the treasure, it's worth it," Farrah declared. "So either you go with us, or you go it alone."

Carmen and Juni gaped at their teammates. Then they raised their eyebrows at each other. Subtly, Juni shook his head at his sister.

And she nodded back. Then she turned to the rest of *El Mejor.*

"You can check out the cactus patch," she said. "Juni and I are going to find another way."

"Fine!" the rest of *El Mejor* blurted out. And then, without even a longing look from Cecilia or a stammering good-bye from Toby, the quartet turned on their heels and flounced away.

Surprised and dejected, Carmen and Juni looked at each other.

"I guess we're on our own," Juni said.

"As usual," Carmen replied with a sigh. She had to admit to herself, though, she was a little relieved. Juni might be annoying occasionally, but at least he was familiar. These other Spy Kids were loose cannons!

Carmen slipped her spy bag strap over her shoulder and began walking toward a forest trail near their grassy hill.

"C'mon," she said. "Let's see if we can get to the bottom of this Spy War."

Carmen and Juni were hiking through the woods. They'd been tromping along for twenty minutes now, looking for the hidden treasure.

"Camp politics," Carmen sighed. "They sure are vicious."

"Yeah!" Juni said. "It reminds me of the old days at school. Before I was a spy."

Back then, the kids had picked on Juni because his hands were all sweaty and warty. He'd always felt scared. Always left out.

But that had all changed when he and Carmen had become spies. After all, nothing boosted your confidence like acquiring kung fu fighting techniques, computer hacking expertise, irrefutable spy logic, and killer smarts.

"It's weird, isn't it," Carmen said, "that this mock mission is so much harder than our real ones? It's like every part of this property has its own special supervillain. I feel like we are getting nowhere."

"Yeah," Juni had to agree. "It's like someone has it out for all us Spy Kids."

Suddenly, Juni heard a voice that made him freeze in his tracks.

"Hey, that's Oscar!" he hissed at Carmen.

Sure enough, Carmen could hear the voice of their camp director.

"He sounds different," she said with a frown. Then, instinctively, she dropped into a crouch. Juni knelt down next to her.

"He's not making jokes," Carmen pointed out.

"Or chuckling the way he usually does," Juni added with a somber nod.

"And he's *sure* not playing folk songs," Carmen said.

Together, the Spy Kids began crawling in the direction of Oscar's voice.

"Okay, so the first day was a bust," they heard him say. "But that's okay. I've waited all this time. I can wait another few days. Heh-heh-heh. I almost feel sorry for the kids. Almost!"

Then Oscar unleashed a belly laugh. Juni shivered. He gazed at Carmen with wide eyes.

"Who's he talking to?" he asked.

Carmen tried to see through the brush. But it was too thick.

"We've gotta get closer," she said.

Juni sighed and began crawling through the dirt.

"I just hope we don't get caught spying on this dude," he whispered. "He's clearly not very sympathetic to Spy Kids."

"Oh, *we* won't get caught," Carmen said. A sudden gleam sparkled in her eye. "Look who I found outside the bathhouse this morning."

Carmen rifled through her canvas spy bag and pulled out a fist-sized golden cage. She opened a little door in the cage and cupped her hands over the opening.

"Gotcha!" she said.

"What is it?" Juni gasped.

Carmen opened her hand to reveal a tiny hummingbird. It was trembly and scared-looking.

"What happened to his beak?" Juni asked. The tip of the tiny bird's long, pointy beak was crumpled up like an accordion.

"He must have flown into the bathhouse window," Carmen said, stroking the bird's little head. "I found him right beneath it. Without his pointy beak, he can't dig into flowers and eat."

"He's gonna die?" Juni cried.

"Not if I can help it!" Carmen said. "I took some sugar from the mess hall. I mixed it with water in an eyedropper. I've been feeding him the stuff all morning and I think he's feeling better."

As she spoke, Carmen pulled the eyedropper out of her pocket. She dripped a few more droplets of sugar water into the hummingbird's ruined beak. He twittered a grateful little song after swallowing the nectar.

"Aw," Carmen said. She sang a perfect hummingbird chirp in return, birdcalls being one of her many spy skills.

"All right, Snow White," Juni said, rolling his eyes. "Does this hummingbird have anything to do with our current situation?"

"'Course," Carmen said. "If we used surveillance equipment from the Gizmo Shed, Oscar might spot it. After all, he probably knows every piece of equipment in there."

"Good point," Juni said with a troubled sigh.

"But Humbert, here," Carmen said, giving the hummingbird's head another stroke, "well, he's all ours. With the exception of this tiny video camera that I'm going to attach to his leg."

Carmen carefully clamped a silver box to the bird's leg. The camera had a fish-eye lens and a minuscule microphone. Carmen calibrated her spy watch to get an instant feed from the camera.

"Okay," Juni said skeptically. "How do you know Humbert here is going to go spy on Oscar for us? It's not like he's OSS-trained or anything."

"We don't," she said. "All I know is, every time I tried to set him free this morning, he flew about fifty feet before he got scared and came back to me for more sugar water."

"Fifty feet, eh?" Juni said. He squinted through the woods. He listened intently to Oscar's faraway voice. He listened like a spy.

"Spy Valley . . . " Oscar was saying. "Best idea . . . why didn't I think of it . . . ?"

Juni turned to his sister.

"Sounds like forty feet to me," he said. "All right, let's let Humbert go!"

"Go on, sweetie," Carmen whispered. She cooed another little hummingbird song to Humbert.

"What is this, a Disney movie?" Juni cracked. But he couldn't resist giving the bird's twitchy head a little pat of his own. Then Carmen tossed Humbert into the air. His wings flapped so fast they blurred. Then he darted straight into the woods.

Juni and Carmen bit their lips and gazed at the screen on Carmen's spy watch.

First they saw nothing on the tiny screen but leaves.

A cluster of flowers came into view and then a large oak tree.

Finally, Oscar appeared. Humbert seemed to be hovering right above him. Over the buzzing of the bird's wings, Carmen and Juni could hear Oscar's voice. They could see him, too. He was pacing back and forth in front of a small cabin. His red eyebrows were wiggling deviously. His bearded mouth was twisted into a smirk. And he was talking a mile a minute—into a mini tape recorder!

"Okay," he dictated into the gadget as he paced back and forth, "once I get my hands on the Atmoso Amulet, the *first* thing I'm going to do is flood California. Never did like California."

Carmen and Juni glanced at each other.

"This is *definitely* not a Disney movie," Juni whispered. The kids listened some more.

"Next," Oscar said, "I think I'll drain the Atlantic Ocean, just a little bit. That way, I can uncover a new barrier island for my personal use. Always did want my own island! Heh-heh-heh."

Juni gasped, but Carmen slapped her hand over his mouth. Oscar was *definitely* a major baddie. If they were caught now, they were doomed!

"I just hope these little twerps come through for me," he said. "Tracking down the Atmoso Amulet has been even harder than I expected. We might lose a Spy Kid or two to this treasure hunt."

Oscar shrugged and said, "Oh well. No matter. The rest of them will stay devoted to me. Some would say, *slavishly* devoted to me. Heh-heh-heh! They'll get me my amulet, eventually."

As Oscar continued to rant, Humbert turned around. He was heading back through the woods. Back toward Carmen and Juni.

But before he reached them, the Spy Kids heard one last snatch of Oscar's manic speech.

"Once the Atmoso Amulet is mine," he said, "I will control all the weather on this earth. Which means . . . I will rule the world! Ah-ha-ha-ha-ha!"

Carmen and Juni sprang to their feet. Humbert flew up to them and alighted on Carmen's shoulder. She gave him a drop of sugar water.

"Good work, Humbert," she said. She unclasped the camera from the bird's tiny leg and slipped Humbert back into his cage.

The kids starting sprinting back through the woods.

"We've gotta warn the others," Juni huffed, "before it's too late!"

CHAPTER 10

When Carmen and Juni got back to the center of camp, the place was deserted.

"Everybody's out treasure-hunting," Juni wailed. "What if something horrible happens to one of the campers?"

Carmen glanced at her spy watch.

"They'll be coming back for lunch in an hour," she said. "We'll talk to them then. Meanwhile, let's figure out what this Atmoso Amulet is!"

The Spy Kids sat beneath a tree, and Carmen booted up her laptop. It only took a few deft keystrokes for her to find a database on the Atmoso Amulet.

"Uh-oh," Carmen said as she scanned the screen.

"What do you mean, 'Uh-oh'?" Juni said.

"This is big," Carmen breathed.

"How big?"

"As big as a hurricane," Carmen said. "Or an avalanche. Or a volcano erup—"

"I get the picture," Juni said. "We've got a bad weather forecast. But what exactly does the Atmoso do?"

"'The keeper of the Atmoso Amulet,'" Carmen read, "'can control weather all over the world. A person in possession of the amulet can simultaneously cause an earthquake at the San Andreas Fault and a heat wave on Mount Everest. The beholder can redirect the paths of rivers, or dry them up entirely. The world is at the mercy of his whims.'"

"What kind of sicko would come up with something like that?" Juni cried. Nervously, he pulled his half-finished lanyard out of his pocket and began weaving it intensely.

"Juni, is this any time to be making jewelry?" Carmen said.

"Hey, usually I snack when I'm nervous," Juni said. "But the OD robots put the kibosh on that when they confiscated my marshmallows. So now I weave."

"Whatever," Carmen said, returning her attention to her computer. "Oooh, I found the answer to your question. What kind of sicko would create such an amulet? 'Three hundred years ago, a parcel of land on the Western side of the continent was occupied by a Native American tribe. The natives were a peace-loving people. But that didn't stop colonizers from brutalizing them and stealing their land. The natives were drummed out of the area and their culture was destroyed.'"

"That's awful!" Juni said.

"'But there was one native who stayed behind,'" Carmen continued to read. "'He was a shaman with extreme, mystical powers. He created the indestructible Atmoso Amulet. And then he began to hex the land with it. Within the space of only five hundred acres, bizarre geographical phenomena erupted. A cactus glade next to a bubbling tar pit. Underwater caverns next to parched desert . . . '"

Carmen stopped reading and looked up at Juni with wide eyes.

"Are you thinking what I'm thinking?" she said.

"Welcome to Spy Valley," Juni said. "Otherwise known as five hundred acres of revenge! Jeez!"

"There's more," Carmen said, returning to the computer. "'Before the witch doctor could do more damage with his amulet, however, another renegade native discovered him. This native was honorable. He refused to let the earth pay for the sins of the colonizers. So he stole the Atmoso from the witch doctor. When he tried to destroy the amulet by smashing it under a rock, the charm spewed sparks, burning the man badly.'"

"I really don't like the sound of this," Juni said. He was weaving his lanyard more frantically now.

"Just wait," Carmen sighed, reading on. "'The best the native could do was to hide the Atmoso where he hoped it would never be found. And just to be safe, he placed a curse upon the charm. All who have attempted to find it have come to extreme harm. It would take someone of great cunning, ingenuity, and stealthy spylike skills to overpower the curse of the Atmoso Amulet. And if that happens, the world as we know it is doomed!'"

"Wow," Juni breathed as Carmen finally finished reading.

"Well, that's good news," Carmen said.

"What?" Juni shouted. "How can you say that?"

"Oscar Zohn," Carmen said, "can't find the Atmoso Amulet without the help of us Spy Kids. But once the other campers find out what he's up to, they'll drop the search. The Atmoso will stay hidden. And we can call the OSS in to arrest this supervillain-masquerading-as-a-cuddly-camp-director."

"You're right!" Juni said. Then he grinned. "I guess Mom and Dad aren't the only ones with breezy assignments!"

"Although . . . " Carmen said, biting her lip. "It

might not be *that* easy. These kids are crazy about Oscar. They're not gonna like it when they learn the truth about him."

"Truth?" said a squeaky voice behind the Cortez kids. "What truth?"

Carmen and Juni spun around. They found themselves staring at Farrah, Cheryl, Toby, and Cecilia. The three girls were all sporting several new earrings and their clothes were full of tiny holes. Toby was wearing a hockey mask and padded clothing from which he was pulling dozens of cactus spines.

"I was the first to go into the cactus patch," he explained to Carmen and Juni.

"And?" Carmen asked, though she already knew the answer. "Did you find the buried treasure there?"

"Does it *look* like we found the treasure?" Cheryl demanded snottily. She flicked a few cactus spikes out of her tangled braids and said, "What about you?"

"We found something much more important than the treasure," Carmen said.

"Yeah," Juni said. "We think there are a few things you should know about Oscar. Or perhaps we should call him 'O. Zohn'!"

As Carmen and Juni launched into the tale of

their morning in the woods, they watched their fellow *El Mejors* stiffen. Then that blank look filled their eyes again. Even Toby's intelligent face went slack and expressionless. Desperately, the Cortez kids kept talking.

Carmen said, "O. Zohn doesn't care if the curse harms Spy Kids. He'll stop at nothing to get that amulet. So *we* have to stop *him*!"

"By spreading the word all over camp," Juni piped up. "The treasure hunt is off. Our new mission? Take down the evil O. Zohn!"

Finally, Carmen and Juni stopped talking. They held their breath and looked at their teammates. They watched the blank looks melt away from their faces.

Please be horrified, Juni thought, crossing his fingers as he waited for the team's reaction.

Please be really mad, Carmen thought, crossing *her* fingers. Help us take down this supervillain.

And please, Juni added, as long as he was hoping against hope, let there be sloppy joes on the lunch menu today.

Finally, the other Spy Kids snapped to life. They *were* horrified. *And* mad. But not at O. Zohn.

"You!" Cheryl cried, pointing a pink-lacquered fingernail at Carmen. "Just because you're not a good enough spy to find the treasure, you want to blame it on poor Oscar."

"How can you say Oscar has it in for us?" Toby added. "He loves his campers!"

"B-but," Juni stuttered, "if he loves his campers, why doesn't he care that this Spy War is killing us?"

"He's just trying to make us stronger," Cecilia yelled.

"B-but," Carmen began, "the curse—"

"What about this?" Farrah said. A dreamy look washed over her face. "Every night, Oscar creates beautiful music and serenades the entire camp. A truly evil man wouldn't be capable of such beauty."

"Yeah," Cheryl said. "Get a clue, Cortezes!"

As a last word, Cecilia stomped on Juni's foot. Then the four Spy Kids stormed away.

Juni grunted as he watched his fellow *El Mejors* heading for the mess hall.

When he looked over at Carmen, she looked worried.

"I'm okay," he said, rubbing his foot with a wince. "Cecilia isn't that big."

"That's not what I'm worried about," Carmen said.

"Oh," Juni replied. "Thanks a lot for the concern."

"No, what I mean is, Cecilia is more loyal to O. Zohn than to you!" she said. "And if you knew anything about girls, which you obviously *don't,* you would know that nothing is more powerful than a girl's crush. Nothing . . . natural, that is."

"So you're saying there's something *super*natural going on here?" Juni said fearfully.

"Well, we're already working with a native curse and a weather-controlling amulet," Carmen said with a shrug. "Why shouldn't O. Zohn get in on the magic, too?"

"What's he *doing* to these guys?" Juni said. He gazed across the campgrounds. More Spy Kids were slumping toward the mess hall. And they all looked as bedraggled and beaten down as *El Mejor.*

"Well, there's one way to find out," Carmen said, putting her finger to her chin. "I think it's time for a little mission of our own."

CHAPTER 11

Later that night, Juni was tossing and turning on his cot in Epsilon Cabin.

"Marshmallows . . . " he moaned. "Chocolate syrup . . . peanut butter and jelly . . . ooohhh, so hungry . . . "

Bzzzzzzzz!

Juni swiped at something fluttering near his nose. Then he flopped over in his bunk and returned to his dream. Somehow, he'd been transported to a Thanksgiving dinner with his parents and Uncle Machete.

"Mmmm," Juni groaned in his sleep. "Sweet potatoes . . . with marshmallows . . . "

Bzzzzzzztttt! Bzzzzzztttt!

Juni's eyes flew open. Then he gasped. He was staring into the tiny black eyes of Humbert! The hummingbird was hovering an inch away from his nose. His wings were buzzing like a tiny jet engine. And attached to his leg was a little video screen monitor. Carmen's face filled the screen. She was wearing a dark knit cap and seemed to be standing next to a tree.

"I thought you'd never wake up," she complained in a whisper. "You were dreaming about food, weren't you?"

"No comment," Juni said with a scowl.

"Whatever," Carmen said. Her eyes shifted back and forth, and then she looked at Juni again. "I'm right behind your cabin. The coast is clear! No OD robots in sight. Get out here on the double. It's mission time!"

"Roger," Juni said. He blinked away his sleep—and his snack-filled dreams.

Time to get into spy mode, he told himself.

Luckily, he was already dressed for spying. When Juni whipped back his blankets, he was fully decked out in his cargo pants, spy vest, gizmo-filled utility belt, and spy watch. He slipped on his own dark knit cap and held out his hand for Humbert. The tiny bird perched on his fingertip. Then—feeling grateful that all his cabin mates were exhausted by the Spy War—Juni slipped out of the cabin without waking anyone.

Humbert jumped off Juni's finger once they were outside and flew straight for a big, tall oak tree about fifty feet away. Juni followed the hummingbird there and found Carmen hiding behind the tree.

"Finally," she whispered, standing up to face her brother. She gave Humbert a few drops of sugar water and waved him into his little cage in her spy bag. Then she turned and started walking deeper into the woods.

"Let's head to O. Zohn's cabin," she said.

"Roger," Juni whispered back.

Stealthily, the Spy Kids began the long hike to O. Zohn's remote hideout. As they crept into the woods, the path got darker and darker.

"It's pitch-black out here," Juni complained. He reached into his spy bag and pulled out a glow stick. He was just about to snap it—and unleash a burst of neon green light—when Carmen grabbed his wrist.

"You can't do that!" she whispered. "With that high-tech gizmo bobbing through the woods, we'd be spotted by a robot easily."

"Okay, how do *you* expect us to find our way?" Juni said. He gazed up at the thick, black canopy of trees. An owl hooted somewhere nearby. He shivered.

"I brought us some bug juice," Carmen said.

She unhooked a canteen from her utility belt and took a big sip. Then she handed the bottle of sticky-sweet fruit punch to Juni.

"Okay," Juni said, taking his own gulp from the canteen. "I'm never one to turn down bug juice, but you didn't answer my question."

"Oh, yes I did," Carmen said. She waggled her fingers at her brother and grinned. Before Juni's incredulous eyes, Carmen's fingertips began to glow. In fact—they flashed! Each fingertip periodically emitted a burst of bright yellow light.

"Your fingertips look like . . . lightning bugs!" Juni gasped.

"Why do you think they call it *bug* juice?" Carmen said. She licked her bright pink lips and took the canteen from Juni's shaking hands. As she recapped it, she said, "Of course, *this* bug juice has an extra kick to it, courtesy of the OSS! I found the mix in the Gizmo Shed."

Juni's own fingertips suddenly sprang to life. They flashed and flickered like energetic fireflies.

"Cooool," Juni breathed, waving his hands around.

"Okay, let's let our fingers do the walking," Carmen said. She held her flashing digits out in front of her. "Here's the path. We should be at

O. Zohn's cabin in about fifteen minutes."

Fourteen and a half minutes later, the Spy Kids saw the glow of O. Zohn's cabin windows ahead of them.

"All the lights are on," Carmen whispered to her brother. "He must still be awake. Be absolutely silent."

"Hello?" Juni said. "You're not the only international superspy on this mission. I know the rules."

"And *I* know that you can be a major klutz," Carmen said back to him. "Just be careful. If O. Zohn catches us, we're doomed."

"Duh," Juni said. But when Carmen wasn't looking, he tiptoed with extra-special care up to one of O. Zohn's windows. Carmen peeked through the window next to his. Both windows looked into O. Zohn's living room.

"Check it out!" Juni hissed to Carmen. "Crunchy, back-to-nature dude, my butt!"

"Shhhh," Carmen hissed. But she also nodded in agreement. O. Zohn's woody log cabin wasn't furnished with the simple furniture, handmade quilts, and cozy antiques you'd expect from such an earthy guy. Instead, it was filled with weather-forecasting satellite feeds, humming computers, and a world map projected from a camera onto a wall. At the far end of the living room was a galley kitchen filled with beakers and test tubes. The only element of O. Zohn's hippie alter ego in the room was his guitar. The Spy Kids spotted it resting on a table.

And then O. Zohn himself, wearing voluminous, cloud-covered pajamas, walked into the living room. He gazed around the room at his weather maps and computers.

"Soon," he said with a cackle. "Soon, you will all be under my spell."

O. Zohn glanced at his guitar.

"Whoops, I almost forgot to charge up my secret weapon!" he said.

He plodded over to his guitar and reached into the sound hole beneath its strings. Pulling a small, black box out of the guitar, he sighed.

"Ah, the Hypn-O-Nar," he said, gazing at the black box fondly. "Could any evil device be more elegant? Simply slip the little box inside my guitar, strum some music, and in minutes, the brats are mine—completely devoted to me."

Unleashing another cackle, O. Zohn slipped the rectangular box into a battery charger on the kitchen counter. Then he yawned luxuriously and turned off the living room light. Pulling his scraggly red hair out of its rubber band, O. Zohn went back out of the room.

Beneath the window, Carmen turned to her brother. Her face was pale with rage.

"That explains *everything,*" she whispered. "Every night O. Zohn's been playing those dorky folk songs to hypnotize us!"

"And it worked!" Juni replied. "Except on you and me. Because we were rocking out to our mini-Walkmans instead."

"That's why everyone's so into O. Zohn," Carmen said, snapping her glowing fingers. "And that's why they won't believe us. But even hypnotized Spy Kids can't argue with hard evidence, can they? We've got to grab that Hypn-O-Nar!"

Juni nodded briskly. Carmen tiptoed around the corner of the little cabin. When O. Zohn's bedroom light clicked off, she rejoined Juni under the living room window.

"Okay, he's gone to sleep," she whispered. "We're going in. I'll guard O. Zohn's bedroom. You grab the box from the battery charger."

"Got it," Juni said with another nod. He pulled his knit cap more firmly over his curls. Both Spy Kids covered their flashing fingertips with black leather gloves. And then, Carmen spritzed the window frame with some Precision-Aim Oil Slick.

"Thanks for the tip, Cheryl and Farrah," Carmen muttered with a wry grin.

"Huh?" Juni whispered.

"Nothing," Carmen said, swallowing a giggle. She gently lifted the window. Perfect—it was totally squeak-free. Carmen dove through the open window with the agility of a cat. She somersaulted silently to her feet and helped Juni climb into the cabin as well. Then she tiptoed to O. Zohn's bedroom door. She peeked into the room. Through the blackness, she could just make out the camp director's hulking form, snoring away beneath a big, puffy blanket.

Carmen nodded at Juni.

He nodded back.

And then, he began to skulk across the living room. The kitchen counter was at the far end of the cramped room. Both Spy Kids held their breath as Juni stepped over electrical wires and phone cords. He shimmied around computer components and sidestepped tables and chairs.

Finally, he reached the Hypn-O-Nar. He hadn't knocked into a single thing! *And* he hadn't made a single noise.

Juni looked across the room at Carmen. He gave her a thumbs-up. And then he stuck his tongue out at her.

"*Who's* a klutz?" he mouthed silently.

All he had to do now was grab the black box and slip it into his spy bag. Juni squinted at the Hypn-O-Nar. A green light on the battery charger flashed on and off to signal that energy was flowing into the gadget.

And in the glow of that green light, Juni spotted something else on the kitchen counter.

Something shiny.

And poofy.

And sweet smelling.

It was a big plastic bag of marshmallows! In fact, it was the very bag of marshmallows that the OD robot had confiscated from Juni on his first day at Spy Valley!

Is there nothing that O. Zohn won't stoop to? Juni fumed silently. He totally cons an entire fleet of Spy Kids. He's trying to take over the world. *And* he steals candy from children.

At the thought of the marshmallows, Juni's stomach rumbled.

He hadn't had a snack for hours.

And he hadn't eaten any sweets for days!

And *these* marshmallows were rightfully his!

What's the harm in grabbing just one little marshmallow? Juni thought. After all, I could use the sugar boost for the hike back to camp. I'll just snag one and then slip O. Zohn's gizmo into my bag.

Juni spun around to make a quick grab for the marshmallow bag.

Unfortunately, he didn't notice the tall stool that was right behind him.

The tall, *wobbly-legged* stool.

The one made of tin.

Just as Juni stuffed a marshmallow into his mouth, the stool toppled over with a loud, metallic clatter.

Carmen gasped.

Juni froze in mid-chew!

And suddenly, a shaft of light spilled out of O. Zohn's bedroom door.

"Who's there?" the supervillain bellowed.

Carmen shot Juni a glance that was part fury, part fear. The Spy Kids were caught!

CHAPTER 12

An instant after O. Zohn's bellow echoed through the cabin, the man himself appeared in his bedroom door.

Despite his baggy, sky-blue jammies bedecked with fluffy clouds, he looked quite threatening.

It might have been the halo of scraggly red hair around his head.

Or the accusing glare in his green eyes.

Or the growl in his voice as he addressed the Spy Kids.

"Carmen and Juni Cortez," he roared. "You are trespassing on your camp director's private property. What's the meaning of this?"

Juni swallowed his marshmallow with a gulp. Then the Spy Kids exchanged a glance. And in a split second, a silent conversation passed between the sister spy and brother spy.

Klutz! Carmen said with her eyes.

Sorry! Juni said with his. Followed by the

question, now how are we gonna get out of this?

Carmen turned to the terrifying O. Zohn. Impulsively, she threw her arms around his big stomach in a bear hug!

"Oh, Oscar," she cried. "I'm so glad you woke up!"

"Huh?" Oscar and Juni blurted at once.

"We were just coming to get you," Carmen said, shooting a wink at Juni.

"Uh, yeah!" Juni piped up. "Because . . . "

"Because?" Oscar growled.

"Because . . . Juni's homesick!" Carmen improvised. "This is his first time away from our mom and dad. And he's miserable without them. He won't stop crying!"

"He won't?" O. Zohn said, giving Juni a sidelong glance.

"Um," Juni murmured. Then he glared at his sister.

"Oh, no," Carmen cried. "There he goes again!"

She glared back at Juni. The Spy Boy looked from Carmen to O. Zohn. He had no choice but to act like the baby Carmen was saying he was! With a sigh of resignation, Juni wailed, "I want my mommy!"

Juni began boohooing up a storm. He heaved

big, fake sobs. He wiped away big, fake tears. He looked at O. Zohn miserably and made his lower lip quiver extra hard.

"Hmmm . . ." O. Zohn said. He looked askance at Carmen, who was wringing her hands with mock concern.

And then O. Zohn huffed irritably.

"Can't a guy rest up for world domination," Carmen heard him mutter under his breath, "without having to deal with sniveling Spy Kids?"

Then she saw O. Zohn's eyes fall on his guitar.

And then a scheming glint entered those eyes. O. Zohn stomped across the living room and grabbed the instrument.

"Listen, Juni," the camp director said as he slung the guitar strap around his neck. "That's a bummer about missing your mommy and all. But you're an OSS spy now. Crocodile tears could get you booted down a level."

O. Zohn quickly strode over to the kitchen counter. Stealthily (but not so stealthily that Carmen and Juni didn't see!) he slipped the Hypn-O-Nar back into the sound hole at the center of the guitar.

Then, he sat on a chair in front of Juni and said, "Now I'm gonna play you one quick lullaby. I *guarantee* you'll feel better afterward. Then you can hightail it back to your cabin and let me get some shut-eye. *Capiche*?"

Juni shot Carmen a panicked look as O. Zohn began to strum his guitar. The evil camp director was siccing his Hypn-O-Nar on them! If they fell under O. Zohn's spell, all the Spy Valley campers were doomed!

O. Zohn began to sing: "Heeeeey, Juni, don't be so sad. Read Mom's e-mail, and you'll feel be-eh-eh-ter."

Carmen's mind raced. She searched her mind for a way to make O. Zohn stop singing.

There has to be, Carmen told herself desperately, some sly spy tactic or brilliant martial arts move or cunning psychological stratagem. Think!

A moment later, Carmen snapped her fingers.

I've got it, she thought. Spy Kids Maneuver #14-K. Works every time.

And what was this #14-K? Uh, that would be screaming really, really loudly.

"Nooooo!" Carmen shrieked.

O. Zohn was so startled, he stopped strumming.

And Juni stopped mock-sobbing.

The evil camp director gazed at Carmen.

"What's wrong *now*?" he asked roughly.

"It's just that . . . " Carmen searched her mind for an explanation. "Your music will only make Juni feel more homesick. Because . . . our dad sings folk songs to us every night."

Juni gaped at his sister. He imagined his dad—with his slick hair and Spanish accent and passion for rock and roll—strumming a guitar and singing lame folk songs. The image was so ludicrous, Juni smiled through his fake tears.

And the more he thought about Gregorio Cortez, the folk singer, the more he smiled. In fact, he started to giggle.

He tried to hold the laugh in and look sad again. But that only made him snort loudly. And *that* made Juni clutch his belly and shriek with laughter.

"Juni!" Carmen said in horror.

Juni couldn't stop laughing. Real tears were streaming from his eyes now. The harder he tried to stop giggling, the more he giggled.

Meanwhile, Carmen was gazing fearfully at O. Zohn. His face was going dark and glowery. And he was muttering to himself again.

Was he onto Carmen and Juni?

And more important, did he know they were onto *him*?!

Carmen stole up behind the camp director just in time to overhear his whisperings.

"Man, kids are weird," he was saying irritably. "When I rule the world, I think I'll exile them all to North Dakota. Meanwhile, I've got nothing to worry about with these two jokers. After all, they got a dose of Hypn-O-Nar at the campfire tonight. Now, if I could just get them out of my cabin . . . "

Carmen heaved a sigh of relief. Then she piped up, "Whoops, guess Juni's feeling better now. We'll get out of your hair, Oscar!"

O. Zohn smiled smarmily.

"You do that," he said, tapping his fingers on his guitar impatiently. "Run along to bed, kiddos. After all, you need your rest if you're going to search extra hard for that treasure tomorrow. You want to win the Spy War, don't you?"

"Um, yes sir," Juni said. He wiped the wetness out of his eyes and jumped out of his chair. O. Zohn led the Spy Kids to the cabin door and a few seconds later, they were outside, waving good-bye. As soon as O. Zohn slammed the door, Carmen and Juni ran down the trail and away from the scene of their spying disaster.

"Man!" Carmen said. She took a swig of bug juice and pulled off her gloves. Her fingertips began to flash and sparkle again. "You really blew it, Juni!"

"I'm sorry," Juni said, hanging his head. "But at least we made it out of there without tipping O. Zohn off. Plus, look what I grabbed while he was leading us to the door."

Juni opened his spy bag and Carmen peered inside.

"Marshmallows!" she said. "Of all the times to be thinking about snacks!"

"Hey, a spy's gotta eat," Juni said. He popped a marshmallow into his mouth.

Carmen glared at her brother. But as she watched him chew the fluffy candy, her mouth started watering.

"All right," she relented. "Give me a couple of those and I'll forgive you."

Juni grinned and passed his sister a handful of marshmallows. As they chomped on the candy and tromped down the trail, Carmen said, "But, we still don't have our evidence—the evil Hypn-O-Nar."

"I know," Juni said sorrowfully. "We *have* to figure out how to get it!"

"The question is, when will we get another chance?" Carmen said.

"Tomorrow?" Juni said through a wide yawn. He

held up his flashing fingertips. He could see Epsilon Cabin in the distance. He couldn't wait to crawl back into his bunk and go back to sleep.

"Yeah," Carmen replied through her own yawn. "We'll think about it in the morning."

"Announcements, an-NOUNCE-ments, an-NOUNCE-ments!"

Carmen's eyes flew open as the familiar, nasal voice of the P.A. system kicked into gear. She groaned and glanced at her spy watch. The wake-up call had come an hour early!

"Ugh," she moaned. "Saving the world on four hours' sleep? No fair!"

As Carmen and her fellow Betas slumped out of their bunks, the announcement continued:

"To give campers more time to fight the Spy War, there will be no breakfast or lunch in the mess hall today. Stop by the clearing in front of the mail station on the way to your mission for meal replacement packets and freeze-dried energy bars. Then you can eat on the run—fun, fun, fun!"

Carmen blinked as the screens retracted with a buzzing sound.

Whoa, she thought. O. Zohn is getting desperate to find that Atmoso Amulet! A camper's bound to get hurt if this pace keeps up.

Carmen had an urge to jump off her bunk and tell all her cabin mates about O. Zohn's evil plan. But one glance at her sullen former teammates Cheryl and Farrah reminded Carmen of the terrible truth—none of these hypnotized Spy Kids were going to believe that Oscar was a bad guy.

The realization made Carmen's shoulders sag.

But, an instant later, her spy spirit kicked in. And so did an idea!

Carmen quickly jumped into her clothes, grabbed her spy bag, and went to track down her brother.

Naturally, she found him near the mail station—a ramshackle, round cabin in which each camper had a secured snail mailbox. Juni was waiting in line for his freeze-dried food, looking glum.

"Oh, hi," he said as Carmen rushed up to him. "What a bummer! I was really hoping for a nice, hot stack of pancakes before we headed back to O. Zohn's cabin."

"Change of plans," Carmen whispered. "We're not going to O. Zohn's cabin."

"What? Why not," Juni hissed back.

Carmen looked shiftily at the other Spy Kids in

line. Many looked superpale. They had gray circles beneath their eyes, and their hands shook with fatigue. But they were also whispering among themselves with weary fervor. They were jabbing at maps with pencils and hacking on their laptops. These were kids on a mission. And nothing Carmen and Juni could tell them about O. Zohn was going to stop them.

The only thing that *would* stop them?

An end to the Spy War.

"Snagging the Hypn-O-Nar will have to wait," Carmen told her brother. "First we have to try to keep these Spy Kids out of danger."

"How?" Juni said with a shrug.

"Juni," Carmen said with determination. "We're going to find the Atmoso Amulet."

CHAPTER 13

Juni gaped at his sister.

Then he began to sputter.

Before he had a chance to say a word though, Carmen grabbed Juni by the elbow and dragged him into the mail station. She shut the door of the musty little cabin and faced her brother.

"There are suspicious Spy Kids everywhere," she said. "Watch what you say."

"Correction," Juni said. "There are bruised, beaten-down, bedraggled Spy Kids everywhere. What makes you think that *we* can find the Atmoso when all of them are totally failing?"

"Because, duh!" Carmen said. "We're the only ones who know that we're searching for the Atmoso!"

Juni slapped his forehead.

"You're right," he said. Then he folded his arms over his chest and nodded. "I'm listening."

"Since the kids aren't going to believe O. Zohn's

evil without hard evidence," Carmen said, "we have to find some other way to stop the treasure hunt."

"So, we'll stop the treasure hunt by finding the treasure!" Juni said, nodding. "Um, how?"

As Carmen pondered a solution, Juni wandered wearily over to his snail mailbox along the station wall.

"Might as well get my mail while we're in here," he said. He placed his palm on a small green screen next to the box.

"Identification: Cortez, Juni, Epsilon Cabin," said a robotic voice in the screen. Juni's mailbox door swung open with a low hiss.

"Contents," the voice continued: "care packages from your mother and from one Machete Cortez."

"Cool!" Juni blurted. He pulled two fat, padded envelopes from his mailbox.

"Uh-huh," Carmen said absently. "So, what do we know about the Atmoso?"

"It's cursed," Juni offered as he tore open one of the envelopes. "It doesn't want to be found."

"Right," Carmen said. "We also know that it can create any weather phenomenon: feast, famine, flood . . . "

"Aw, man," Juni said, peeking into one of the envelopes. "Mom sent me chocolate bars and peanut butter crackers. The OD robots are gonna smell these snacks and snatch them away, for sure."

Juni pulled a few black cartridges out of the envelope.

"And video game plug-ins for my laptop," Juni sighed. "As if I have time for fun and games when I have a world to save. Again!"

Carmen totally wasn't listening to Juni's pity party. Because she'd just figured something out!

"Wait a minute!" she said. "A weather amulet that doesn't want to be found. It's simple! All the Atmoso has to do is protect itself with . . . mega-lightning bolts or a mini-tornado or something like that."

Juni looked up from his care package and raised his eyebrows.

"As always, I hate to agree with you," he said, "but you're right! If we can find a spot on the campgrounds with really bizarre weather patterns . . . "

"*X* marks the spot!" Carmen announced.

Juni jumped up and down so hard that a chocolate bar flew out of his envelope.

"Okay, but we're dealing with five hundred acres here," he said. "How are we going to pinpoint one little pocket of stormy weather?"

"Hmmm," Carmen said again. "I guess we could check out your scale model again. Maybe there are some clues there."

"Maybe," Juni said with an unenthusiastic shrug.

As he spoke, he stashed their mom's care package in his spy bag and tore open Uncle Machete's envelope. He pulled out a note and read out loud to Carmen:

"Dear Juni,

How's camp? I'm a little jealous of you and Carmen! As a boy, I spent every summer at science camp. What fun! And of course, it made me the inventor I am today!"

Juni paused and gave Carmen a baleful look. "Everybody," he complained, "gets to go to a cool camp, it seems, except for us!"

Juni continued to read his uncle's letter:

"I know camp isn't camp without a care package. So here's a Machete Cortez gadget—hot off the presses! I bet it'll come in handy on those long hiking trips!

Love,

Uncle Machete"

Juni dug eagerly into the envelope. He pulled out a silver disk with a ring of rainbow-colored lights on its edges. He looked at a little card dangling from the disk.

"A Meteorological Mystic," he murmured.

Finally, Carmen snapped to attention. She ran to Juni's side.

"Meteorological Mystic?" she gasped. "Perfect!"

"Huh?" Juni said.

"Hello, Mr. I-got-a-C-in-English-class," Carmen said. "Meteorological means weather-related. And a mystic is sort of a fortune-teller."

Eagerly, Carmen read the instructions.

"'Excellent for those long missions across unfamiliar terrain,'" she read, "'the Meteorological Mystic will help you prepare. Just point the gadget in the direction of travel and it will predict the area's weather patterns.' *Perfecto!*"

"Let's go!" Juni cried. He stuffed the Meteorological Mystic into his spy bag. Then the Cortez kids skulked out of the mail station and snuck to a hilltop far away from the cabins. They could see small troops of Spy Kids tromping wearily into the woods, across the meadows, and down to the lakefront. As soon as everyone had dispersed, Juni pulled out the Meteorological Mystic. When he flipped it on, the gizmo emitted a low humming noise and its jelly-bean-colored lights pulsed lightly.

Carmen glanced at the instructions again and looked toward the northern border of the camp.

"Let's start there," she said. "Just point the Meteorological Mystic in that direction, then press that big, purple button in the middle of the dial."

Juni pointed.

Then he pressed.

And both Spy Kids held their breath as the Meteorological Mystic began to vibrate and burble. The rainbow lights stopped pulsing and started flashing.

And finally, a strip of paper began to unfurl from the bottom of the gadget. When the printout finished, Juni grabbed it.

"Huh," he said dejectedly. "It just says, 'sunshine, partly cloudy.'"

"Nothing unusual about that," Carmen said. "Why don't you point it toward the tar pits."

Juni complied. And again, the Spy Kids waited breathlessly while the Meteorological Mystic flashed, whirred, and spat out a strip of paper.

"'Sunshine, partly cloudy!'" Juni read again.

"Okay," Carmen said with a shrug. "Try the cactus patch."

"'Sunshine, partly cloudy.'"

"The swimming hole?"

"'Sunshine, partly cloudy.'"

"The dandelion meadow? The parched desert? The underwater caverns?"

"'All sunshine, partly cloudy,'" Juni said dejectedly. "Maybe Uncle Machete didn't iron out all of this gizmo's glitches!"

Carmen took the Mystic from her brother's hands. She spun around and surveyed the idyllic campgrounds once more. And then . . . in the distance . . . over Spy Valley's southeastern corner, she saw a single, dark gray cloud.

"Hmmm," she said. She pointed the gadget at the cloud.

The gizmo hummed. It shuddered. It twitched and jumped and flashed. And then, it spat out an extra-long strip of paper.

"'Sunshine, partly cloudy . . .'" Carmen read. Then her eyes went wide—"' . . . at ten-o-six A.M. Followed immediately by two minutes of thunderstorms. Hurricane warning from ten-thirteen through ten-twenty-four. Five-minute heat wave to follow . . . '"

The list went on. But Carmen didn't need to read any further. She looked at her brother with a big grin.

"Juni," she said. "I think we've got our Atmoso."

"Yes!" Juni said, pumping his fist. "Does the Mystic give us exact coordinates?"

"Yup. We're going . . . " Carmen paused and her face fell. "Oh, it's four whole miles away."

"It's gonna take forever to get there on foot!"

Juni complained. "Let's take rocket-powered back-packs."

"Too visible," she said. "No, I think we need to stay close to the ground."

As she spoke, she pulled a couple of gadgets from her spy bag. The gizmos consisted of conical caps attached to a couple of shoulder straps. Grimly, she handed one to Juni.

"As close to the ground as possible," she added.

"What's this thing called?" Juni said as he slung the straps over his shoulders and buckled the cap beneath his chin.

"The Earthworm," Carmen said. "I grabbed it from the Gizmo Shed before I came to get you at the mail station. I thought it might come in handy."

"Oh," Juni said. He pressed a few buttons on the chin strap. "How's it work?"

"You'll see," Carmen said. She pressed a few buttons of her own. Then she gasped, "Whoa!"

Juni gaped as Carmen's conical hat sprouted a huge propeller. As it began spinning wildly, Carmen lost her balance and flopped onto her stomach. Then the propeller plunged forward. Carmen began whizzing through the grass and dirt toward the site of the Atmoso Amulet.

Next, Juni felt his own cap begin to vibrate. His

propeller had sprouted! Then he, too, tipped over and began whizzing along the ground.

"Ptew, ptew, ptew," Juni sputtered, spitting out the dirt clods, pebbles, and grass blades that kept hitting him in the teeth. He felt his forehead become encrusted with plants. His hair became matted with mud. His clothes turned a uniform shade of brown.

But on the bright side, in three minutes the messiest ride on earth had ended. And Carmen and Juni found themselves inside a lush grove.

"Ugh!" Carmen said. She lurched to her feet, scraping twigs, dirt, and grass off her arms and legs. "That was awful."

"Awfully fun!" Juni said, once he'd recovered from the wild ride. "Like I always say, the best thing about being a spy is getting dirty without getting in trouble!"

Juni looked around the grove. "Well, it worked. I don't see a soul. Nobody followed us here."

Carmen consulted her spy watch's satellite tracking system.

"Looks like we landed in the right place," she said. "We're at Spy Valley's southeastern corner."

Juni looked up through the thick circle of trees at the sky. Directly above the grove were a few clouds and alternating beams of sunlight.

"Sunshine, partly cloudy," Juni said with a nod. "Let's see what else they've got."

As if on cue, a giant thunderclap rocked the glade. Then, an instant rush of rain began to pummel the Spy Kids.

"Well, we did need a shower," Juni said as the thunderstorm rinsed them clean of mud and muck.

The rain ended abruptly.

"'Two-minute thunderstorm,'" Carmen read off the printout. "Looks like we're in the right place."

"Great!" Juni said. "Except . . . wasn't the next thing on that list a hurricane warning?"

Again, Juni spoke and the weather responded. This time, wet winds slammed into the spies. They struggled to remain on their feet.

"Gotta find some shelter!" Juni gasped.

Carmen swiped rain out of her eyes and peered around the dark and stormy grove. Then she pointed to an opening in the trees.

"Over there," she shouted. "I see a cave!"

Clutching each other for support, the kids found their way to the dark, tunnel-like cave. When they got inside, they slumped to the ground.

"Whew!" Juni said. "That Atmoso isn't kidding. Harsh weather."

He looked around the little cave. It was dank and muddy and smelled like really bad breath.

"Of course," he added, "it's not much better in here."

"Yeah," Carmen said as she touched the cave wall gingerly. "It's totally slimy."

Grrrrrrrr.

"And noisy," Juni pointed out.

GRRRRRRRR!

Carmen jumped and gazed around the cave. The ceiling seemed to be vibrating! And for that matter, so was the floor!

"Um . . . Juni?" she said.

"Yeah," Juni replied tremulously.

"I think that noise might be—"

GROOOWWWWRRR!

Suddenly, the ceiling started to close in on the Spy Kids! And the growling got even louder.

"This is no cave!" Carmen screamed. "We're in the mouth of some kind of monster. Run!"

CHAPTER 14

Carmen and Juni made a dash for the mouth of the . . . mouth. Carmen dove through the opening and did a somersault across the damp ground.

She turned, expecting to see her brother tumbling to safety next to her.

But he wasn't there!

"Juni!" Carmen cried fearfully. She spun around. Then she gasped.

She was staring down at a legless creature so big, it looked like a small mountain. Its skin was as brown and slithery as a mud slide. Its squinty eyes looked like gray and black rocks topped by bushy, shrublike eyebrows.

And its cavelike mouth was closing! Juni was still lying on the floor—or rather, the tongue—inside.

"I fell," Juni cried. He struggled to find his footing on the slick, slimy tongue.

"Don't worry about getting up," Carmen screamed. "Crawl!"

She began to scramble toward the monster, her hand outstretched to her brother. But before she could reach him, the mouth closed completely!

On Juni!

"Carrrrrr-mennnn!" Juni cried from inside the monster's mouth.

"Juni!" Carmen screamed back. She began tearing gadgets off her utility belt, searching desperately for a weapon that might make the mud monster open its trap. But before she could find anything, the mud monster unleashed a roar—a great, widemouthed roar.

A very slimy, very shaky Juni tumbled out of the monster's mouth. He was holding his self-flaming stick. Its ember was burning at full blast. Carmen grabbed Juni by the hand and dragged him away from the still bellowing mud monster.

Juni fell to his knees, breathing hard. Carmen slumped next to him, Luckily, the brief hurricane had just ended. Now they were bathed in the sunshine of the five-minute heat wave.

"I burned the roof of his mouth with the self-flaming stick," Juni explained as soon as he caught his breath. He folded the stick up and gave the mud monster a dirty look.

The monster responded with another angry

roar. But there was nothing it could do to them.

"That was close," Carmen said. She squeezed water and slime out of her hair. "Too close. We have to make sure none of the other Spy Kids find this place. They might not be as lucky as you were."

"You're right," Juni said, stumbling to his feet. "But we can't just sit here, guarding the grove! We've still got to get to O. Zohn's black box and the Atmoso Amulet."

"Yeah . . . " Carmen said. She bit her lip. As she pondered, she began gathering up the gadgets that she'd dropped on the ground earlier. She clipped her laser cutter and high-beam flashlight and grabber cable to the belt. But when she picked up the last gizmo—a small box with a round lens bulging out of it—she cried out, "This is perfect."

"What's that?" Juni said. He trotted up to take a look. "A hologram projector? Carmen, I'm as much of a TV hound as the next kid, but is this really the time to be watching cartoons?"

"Yeah!" Carmen said. "But not for fun. Watch!"

She ran to the edge of the grove of trees. Looking up, the kids could already see the blazing light of the heat wave being replaced by billowing gray clouds. Snow clouds! While Juni gaped at the weird weather, Carmen put her gadget on the ground and pulled a little keyboard out of its base. She typed in some instructions and hit PLAY.

Instantly, the clouds, the snow, and the entire glade disappeared! Juni gasped as it turned into a meadow filled with wildflowers and butterflies.

"You cloaked the grove in a gigantic hologram," Juni said. "Wow!"

"If you can't beat it," Carmen answered with a grin, "hide it."

"For now," Carmen said, "we've still got to thwart O. Zohn!"

Juni nodded and pulled his Earthworm out of his spy bag.

"Now that we've found the site of the Atmoso Amulet," he sighed, "it's time to track down the Hypn-O-Nar."

While the other campers spent the rest of the day desperately seeking buried treasure, Carmen and Juni hunted for the Hypn-O-Nar.

On their way back to Spy Valley, they stopped by O. Zohn's empty cabin and peeked through the window again. The Hypn-O-Nar charger was empty. And the guitar was AWOL, too.

"O. Zohn must have his guitar—and his evil gizmo—with him," Juni said dejectedly.

"So," Carmen said with grim determination, "*we* find O. Zohn."

They headed back to the main camp. They stopped at the mess hall and peered into the empty dining room. No O. Zohn.

They went to the lakefront. He wasn't there either.

Nor was he in the infirmary, the arts and crafts hut, the Gizmo Shed, *or* the lodge.

"Man, for a big guy, that O. Zohn sure is elusive," Juni complained as he and Carmen tromped through the woods. They were headed back to Epsilon Cabin to check out Juni's Spy Valley model.

"I know," Carmen sighed. "What a pai—"

Before she could finish her sentence, Carmen froze. Then she yanked Juni behind a tree and whispered, "Do you hear that sound?"

Juni cocked his head.

Snarf-snarf-snarf.

He nodded. About twenty feet away, something was making a wet, mushy, munchy noise. The kids held their breath and listened some more.

Snarf-snarf-snarf.

Suddenly, Juni stifled a gasp.

"I know that noise!" he whispered. "That's definitely the sound of someone snacking!"

"Only you," Carmen whispered, "could turn pigging out into a spy skill."

Juni stuck his tongue out at Carmen. She ignored it and said, "Let's check this out."

Using all their stealthy spy skills, Carmen and Juni crept from tree to tree. The snacking sounds got louder. Finally, they crouched together behind a thick tree trunk. They were as close to the snacker as they could safely get. Carefully, Juni unhooked his extendible mini-periscope from his utility belt. Then he put one end of the gadget to his eye and pressed a button. Inch by silent inch, the periscope's lens crept around the tree trunk. Finally, Juni could see something!

It was a man's back—a big wide back, dressed in an orange Spy Valley T-shirt.

Juni raised his sights a bit. His eyes widened.

The man had a frowsy, red ponytail. And fleshy, freckled arms.

It was O. Zohn!

Make that a chocolate-smeared O. Zohn! The evil camp director was sitting on a log gorging himself. In his lap was a canvas bag, brimming with chocolate bars, cupcakes, and other treats the OD robots had confiscated from campers.

Juni felt a vein begin to throb in his temple.

His hands clenched into fists.

And he trembled with rage.

So *all* the goodies confiscated by the OD robots went straight into O. Zohn's belly! The man really *was* pure evil!

Without a word, Juni handed the periscope to Carmen. She took a look. And when she looked back at Juni, she was smiling.

"Did you see what he's got?" she whispered.

"Yeah!" Juni whispered indignantly. "Treats that rightfully belong to us campers!"

"*Besides* that," Carmen said, giving Juni a little thunk on the head. "His guitar! It's next to him!"

"Oh," Juni said. "Well, like you said, it's right next to him. So how do we get to the Hypn-O-Nar?"

Carmen's face lit up. Then she grabbed Juni's spy bag.

"Juni," she said. "We're going fishing!"

Then the Spy Kids put their heads together and came up with a plan. A few seconds later, they were ready to put it into action.

While O. Zohn continued his sugary feast, Juni pulled some gloves from his spy vest. He slipped them on and pressed a button. Sharp, metal hooks sprang from the gloves' fingertips. Juni sank the hooks into the tree bark and started climbing.

Meanwhile, Carmen slunk through the trees toward a new hiding place about thirty feet in front of O. Zohn.

Juni reached the top of the tree and perched on a sturdy branch.

Carmen ducked into a bank of shrubs.

And then, the Spy Kids looked at each other.

Carmen raised her eyebrows in question.

Juni took off his gloves and pulled his lanyard out of his pocket. He fiddled with the metal loop at the lanyard's end. When he found a split in the silver ring, he pried it open. Then he flashed his sister a thumbs-up. He was set.

With that, Carmen reached into Juni's spy bag. She grabbed one of his chocolate bars and tossed it.

O. Zohn looked up from his snack stash. He'd spotted the candy!

"Huh?" he grunted. "Hmmm."

Juni held his breath and waited. Then—yes!—O. Zohn hauled his portly self to his feet. He began to lumber down the forest trail.

"What's that?" he mused. "Could it be . . . a peanut-butter crunch bar? My favorite!"

Mine, too! Juni thought with a scowl. Then he shook his head. He didn't have time to mourn for his munchies. He had only seconds to complete his part of the mission.

He lowered his lanyard down, down, down toward O. Zohn's guitar. Luckily, the evil camp director had left it propped against the log.

Juni slipped the lanyard's split ring through the guitar strings and into the instrument's sound hole. Then he glanced down the forest trail. O. Zohn was just bending down to pick up the peanut-butter crunch bar. Juni had to hurry!

Gingerly, he tried to snag the Hypn-O-Nar. He jiggled the lanyard around. He felt the ring hit something! It had to be the evil gadget! Juni moved the lanyard in a scooping motion, then pulled.

But when the ring emerged from the sound hole, it was empty.

Gritting his teeth, Juni went fishing again.

Meanwhile, Carmen was still crouched in the bushes. She was watching O. Zohn with a curled lip. He'd unwrapped the peanut-butter crunch bar and devoured it in three bites.

Now, he was turning around. He was getting ready to return to his perch on the fallen log!

Carmen glanced at O. Zohn's guitar. Juni's lanyard was still dangling inside it! Clearly, her brother hadn't hit pay dirt yet. Desperately, she grabbed another candy bar and winged it at the camp director.

Thwack!

The candy bar hit him square in the back of his woolly head! Carmen cringed.

Real subtle, she scolded herself. She held her breath as O. Zohn looked around wildly. Then he spotted the chocolate bar at his feet.

"Raspberry caramel deluxe!" he cried, scooping the candy off the ground. Then he peered into the trees again. When he couldn't spot anybody, he shrugged. "My beloved OD robots must have found another stash of sweets! Sorry, Spy Kid suckers!"

With that, O. Zohn began devouring the raspberry caramel deluxe bar. Carmen heaved a sigh of relief. O. Zohn thought this was just another confiscated sweet. And she'd bought Juni another minute or so of fishing time.

And he was going to need every second of it.

He was now dipping his lanyard ring into the guitar for the third time. He was sweating.

And shaking.

And the lanyard was jiggling like mad.

Oh, no! Juni thought. *My jangly nerves are going to wreck the mission!*

But no sooner had the thought crossed his mind than he felt the ring hit something solid.

He gave the lanyard a little tug. It went taut. Juni

had hooked the Hypn-O-Nar!

He yanked the string upward and almost yelled with joy as the little black box zipped into his hand.

Good thing he used his other hand to stifle his shout. At that exact moment, O. Zohn swallowed the last bite of the raspberry caramel deluxe bar. Now, he began lumbering back to his log.

"Mmmmm," the evil camp director muttered. "Just one more and I'll head back to camp. Time to see if any of those Spy Kids have found my Atmoso Amulet yet!"

Carmen slunk back to Juni's tree. She met her brother just as he finished his climb down the trunk. The kids sneaked back down the trail. When they were far enough away from O. Zohn, Carmen paused on the forest trail and grinned at Juni.

"Good job," she said. "How'd you do it?"

"Video game plug-ins!" Juni said. "They really *do* improve your hand-eye coordination."

"Cool," Carmen said. "Now all we need to do is find the other campers and show them this horrible Hyp—"

"Freeze, campers!"

"Aigh!" Juni cried. He spun around to face their surprise visitor.

"Oh, no!" he cried.

"OD you mean," Carmen said bitterly.

Carmen and Juni were staring down one of the On-Duty robots: a robot charged with making sure no Spy Kids veered from their treasure-hunting duties. A robot that could sniff out an illicit snack like the remaining chocolate bar still in Carmen's pocket from a hundred feet away.

"You're in big trouble . . ."—the robot paused while its hardware beeped and whirred—"Carmen Cortez of Beta Cabin and Juni Cortez of Epsilon."

Juni and Carmen both raised their hands over their heads as the flashing, beeping robot rolled toward them. Its claws were poised to grab their shirt collars.

"Busted!" Juni whispered.

"Not if I can help it," Carmen muttered back. Then she planted a sad, sympathetic look on her face and looked the robot in its mechanical eyes.

"You caught us," she sighed. "Congratulations. Are we your first renegade campers of the day?"

The robot's head whirred as it tilted to look at Carmen.

"Yes," the OD said, heaving a heavy mechanical sigh of its own. "The other campers are too busy treasure-seeking to do anything bad. They really listen to Camp Director Zohn!"

"Oh," Carmen said. Her voice dripped with compassion. "So, this job must be really boring."

"I am a robot," the OD said. "I do not get bored. I do my job—look for Spy Kids sneaking snacks and shirking duties. Every day. Day after day."

"Okay . . . " Carmen said. "So, you don't get bored."

But her tone said she was unconvinced. She lowered a hand from above her head and placed it on the OD's shoulder hinge.

"But wouldn't it be nice," she suggested, "if you had something to help you pass the time? Something . . . fun?"

"Fun?" the robot said. It cocked its mechanical head again.

"Fun!" Carmen said. Suddenly, she reached into Juni's spy bag. She pulled out three small cartridges and waved them beneath the OD's nose.

"Hey . . . " Juni protested. "Not my video games, too!"

"You don't have time for them," Carmen said through clenched teeth. "And besides, this is more important."

Meanwhile, the OD robot was looking at the cartridges.

"Is that . . . Tetris?" its robotic voice said hopefully. "And, oh! Tony Hawk's Pro Skater 2?"

"Yes, it is!" Carmen said with a gleam in her eye. She waved the plug-ins enticingly. "Wanna play?"

The OD robot waved its claw sheepishly.

"No, no," it said wanly. "I must do my job."

"Oh, loosen up," Carmen said. She reached over and popped Pro Skater 2 into a slot in the robot's belly. A screen erupted in the middle of the robot's face. A scraggly skater kid began kick-flipping around the screen. The OD robot reached for the control buttons installed in its wrist.

Carmen and Juni began to inch away.

The robot paid no notice. It was too busy trying to make the skater on its screen skim down a banister into a parking lot.

"He's in the zone," Juni whispered to his sister. "Let's make a break for it!"

With that, the Spy Kids turned and ran! They'd escaped the OD robot!

"Now we just need to show the other Spy Kids this Hypn-O-Nar," Juni declared. He gripped the black box in his fist. "We'll do it the first chance we get!"

CHAPTER 15

The first chance Carmen and Juni got was the next morning. By the time the other campers had slumped back from another unsuccessful day of treasure-seeking, they were so exhausted they'd flopped right into their bunks.

So, immediately after the wake-up announcement the next day, Carmen and Juni hurried to the breakfast line near the mail station. Carmen had stashed their evidence—the evil Hypn-O-Nar—in her spy bag. When the Cortezes arrived at the line, they found their fellow campers looking more bleary-eyed and bedraggled than ever. But they were also raring to go.

Juni scanned the line. He spotted the Powers, the Tigers, and a bunch of other teams the Cortez kids had become familiar with. But then, Juni frowned.

"Hey," he wondered, "where's the rest of *El Mejor*?"

"Didn't you hear?" said a voice behind them.

Carmen and Juni turned around. It was Carmen's cabin mate, Beth. She was sporting a nasty scrape on her knee and the beginnings of a black eye. She was also brimming with gossip.

"Hear what?" Carmen asked her friend.

"*El Mejor* think it's found the treasure!" Beth said.

"What?!" Carmen and Juni blurted.

"I know," Beth said sympathetically. "You must be pretty bummed that you broke away from the winning team. I heard it was all Toby's doing."

"Really?" Juni asked.

"Uh-huh," Beth said, nodding earnestly. "Somehow, he tracked down the treasure under some really weird weather patterns. He found it even though there was a hologram cloaking its location! He's a genius, that Toby."

"Beth," Carmen said, grabbing her friend by the shoulders. "Please tell me. When did all this happen?"

"Just a few minutes ago," Beth said. "*El Mejor* skipped breakfast to get a jump on the treasure hunt. When they found its location, Farrah called one of the Powers with her cell phone to tell him about it. She was psyched!"

And the Cortez kids were bummed. Dashing away from the mail station, they whipped their Earthworms out of their spy bags. Then they quickly burrowed toward the hidden forest glade. They arrived a few minutes later, spitting out dirt and grass. The area still looked like a breezy, pretty meadow. But as Juni pulled the Earthworm off his head, he grabbed Carmen's arm.

"Look!" he said. He pointed at a spot off to the left.

There was a hole in the meadow hologram! It was right near the grass, about two feet wide and two feet tall—just big enough for a Spy Kid to fit through. Carmen and Juni ran over to the hole and bent over to peer through it.

They saw a few weather-battered tree trunks.

They saw hurricane-smashed leaves and snow-sodden dirt.

And they heard—high-pitched screams!

"That's Cheryl and Farrah!" Carmen cried. "Come on!"

Carmen, then Juni, dove through the hole into the grove. As they began running toward the screams, they were pelted by marble-sized hail.

"Ow! Ow! Ow!" the Cortezes cried as the hail-stones thunked them on their heads. But they couldn't take cover. It was hero time!

And boy, did Farrah and Cheryl need a hero. When Carmen and Juni found them, they were both struggling within the mouth of the mud monster! The creature had swallowed both girls up to their waists. And, though the Spy Girls were clawing at the ground so hard that all their press-on nails had popped off, the monster wasn't letting go. He growled and grunted and hung on tight.

A mud-smeared Toby was nearby, slingshotting sticks and stones at the monster. But the weapons had no impact on the burly beast.

"Got your self-flaming stick?" Carmen asked Juni, wincing as another hailstone thunked onto her head.

When Juni pulled the stick out of his bag and unfurled it to its full, glow-tipped length, Carmen saw something else in Juni's satchel—a puffy, plastic bag. She grabbed it!

"My marshmallows!" Juni said, trying to grab the bag back. "Nooooo!"

Carmen shook him off. She grabbed the self-flaming stick and plunked a few marshmallows onto the ember. Instantly, the candies started getting gooey and toasty.

When they were fully roasted, Carmen stood out

of reach of the mud monster and yelled at him, "Hey, dirtbag."

The mud monster stopped growling. He looked at Carmen with interest. Or maybe it was hunger.

"You know, those girls aren't very nice," Carmen told the monster.

"Um, Carmen," Cheryl said, looking desperately at her cabin mate. "I know we were really, really mean to you. But you wouldn't stoop to feeding us to this monster, would you?"

"Please, Carmen," Farrah sobbed. "I'm so sorry about the mosquitoes. And the oil slick. And all the horrible things I said about you to the Deltas. . . ."

"What?" Carmen gasped. "Of all the low-down, nasty . . . "

Fuming, Carmen glared at Farrah and Cheryl. She was tempted to let the mud monster eat them. But one glance at her brother reminded her of the Cortez code—honor first, personal disputes second.

So, she merely curled her lip at the Spy Girls and turned her attention back to the mud monster.

"Listen," she said to the monster. "All I'm saying is, why eat something so *sour* when you can have something *sweet* instead?"

Carmen lobbed the gooey marshmallows

toward the mud monster.

His rocky eyes widened. His nostrils flared as he sniffed the treat. And then, he opened his mouth wide to catch the marshmallows—releasing his screaming captives.

Farrah and Cheryl scrambled away from the monster. As they thanked Carmen weepily, Carmen winked at the creature.

"Good mud monster," she said. Then she toasted a few more marshmallows and tossed them to him. The creature's growls had turned into purrs of contentment.

"Yes!" Juni said, bounding up to Carmen's side. Toby joined them, patting Carmen on the back.

But their celebration didn't last long.

"Hey," Carmen said, looking around as she folded up the self-flaming stick. "Where's Cecilia?"

"Aaaaaiiiigggh! Help meeeeeeeee!"

As the squeaky scream reverberated through the glade, Juni gasped.

"*That* would be Cecilia," he said. He looked at the far end of the grove. The scream had come from over there. But there was no sign of the young spy. "We've gotta find her."

Carmen nodded and started to beckon to the

other Spy Kids. But then she looked them over. Cheryl and Farrah were slimy with mud monster spit. They were still sobbing and trembling. Toby was sticking his chin out bravely, but after his battle with the monster, he was weak and shaky.

What's more, they were all still being pelted by hail.

Carmen shook her head. These spies would be no good in a fight. In fact, they might be a liability! Carmen thought fast. She addressed the bedraggled *El Mejors.*

"Word's gotten around camp about Toby's find. We don't want anyone else to get in here and get hurt," she told them. "So I need you guys to go guard the hole in the hologram. Don't let any other Spy Kids in."

"Yes, Carmen," Farrah said meekly.

"Whatever you say," Cheryl said.

Carmen couldn't help but smile. I like the sound of *that,* she thought.

"Okay," she said, giving the trio a wave. "Juni and I are going after Cecilia. See you soon!"

The Cortez kids dashed around the still-purring mud monster. They followed the sounds of Cecilia's screams. But the more they chased her, the farther away she seemed to get—and the crazier the weather got. The Spy Kids found themselves pummeled by hail and snow and rain, all at once!

"We must be getting closer to the Atmoso Amulet," Juni gasped as they fought through the punishing precipitation.

"Maybe this'll help us," Carmen said through gritted teeth. She pulled the Meteorological Mystic out of her spy bag and pointed it at the sky. The gadget hummed and vibrated, then spat out a damp wad of paper. Smoothing the printout on her leg, Carmen read, "'Flash flood, followed by a cyclone.'"

"That doesn't sound good," Juni called out over the howling wind.

But then, suddenly, the wind stopped.

"Hey," Juni said. "Is this the calm before an even worse storm?"

"Before a flash flood!" Carmen cried out. She looked around and braced herself for a rush of freezing water. But no water came. In fact, the air was filling with sparkly sunshine.

And more sparkly sunshine.

And *more.* In fact, within a few seconds the kids were besieged by darting dots of light! The sparks surrounded them, zipping in front of their eyes and nipping at their noses. They stung their arms and burned their legs.

"Ah, get 'em off me," Juni cried, slapping at the sparks.

"It's like we're being attacked by flashbulbs!" Carmen screeched. She snapped her fingers.

"Oh, I get it—a *flash* flood," she said with a frown. "*Very* punny. I've *had* it with these Atmoso antics. When I get ahold of that amulet, I'm gonna smash it to smitherEEEEENNNS! Whoa!"

Before Carmen could finish her rant, the weather changed again. Suddenly, she was being swept into a muddy chute by a rush of water. It swept her right off her feet!

"Oh, no!" Juni cried. "That must be the cyclone! WHOA!"

Before Juni could escape, the cyclone whooshed him away, too.

"Aaaaaaahhhh!" Juni screamed as the chute turned left, then right, then shot straight down. It even took him into a loop-de-loop.

"This roller-coaster ride would be kinda fun," Juni said to himself, "if only I knew where it was going to end uuuuupppp!"

Make that down. And down and down and down until—

Plop!

"Ooof," Juni grunted. The chute had spat him out into a dark, muddy, underground cave. Next to him, Carmen was already lurching to her feet, swiping muddy water out of her eyes. She reached down and helped Juni up. They squinted into the dark gloom of the cave.

"I can't see a thing," Carmen complained. Then she remembered she'd stashed Juni's self-flaming stick in her pocket. She pulled it out and unfurled it. She swept the glowing end out in front of her. The cave filled with dusky light. Carmen looked around. Then she gasped.

"Cecilia!" she said.

"Mmmmm-mmm-mmm!" Cecilia grunted.

The terrified Spy Girl couldn't speak, because her mouth was covered.

Covered by a large hand.

The hand of Oscar Zohn!

And what was that dangling from a glinty, golden chain in O. Zohn's other hand?

The Atmoso Amulet!

"Hello, Cortezes," O. Zohn said.

"Hello . . . O. Zohn," Juni said with a scowl. "We're going to ask you nicely to let Cecilia go."

"Yeah," Carmen said. She crouched into a kung fu fighting stance. "And if you don't, then we'll ask you *not* so nicely."

"The choice is yours," Juni said, holding up his own fists.

O. Zohn merely laughed again.

And then he did something very unexpected.

He let Cecilia go! As soon as O. Zohn unhanded her, Cecilia began to shriek in terror. Rolling his eyes, the evil camp director shoved her away. Cecilia ran to cower behind Juni.

"Take her," O. Zohn said. "I don't need a hostage any more. After all—I have the amulet."

He does have a point, Carmen thought. In the wall behind O. Zohn, she could spot a little niche. Inside the niche was an ornately carved wooden stand, topped by a dusty silk pillow.

That must be where the amulet lay for three-hundred years, Carmen thought. And now, O. Zohn has centuries of accursed power in his hand. His very *evil* hand.

How, she thought, are we going to stop him?

Clearly, O. Zohn was thinking the same thing. With an arrogant smirk, he hung the ancient amulet around his neck. Instantly, little lightning bolts began sparking out of his fingertips. His red hair stood on end. And the earth around his feet began to freeze into a crackly ice patch!

"Any final words," O. Zohn snarled, "before I use my amulet to wash you three out of my sight?"

"Just a few," Juni growled.

Carmen glanced over at her brother and gasped. While she'd been pondering a solution, Juni had been stringing one together. Literally!

He'd grabbed a stick off the cave floor. Then he'd unraveled his purple and yellow lanyard. He'd looped the lanyard strings up and down the stick, anchoring it on various twigs and knots.

He'd made a guitar! Yes, it was the crudest, most ridiculous-looking guitar! But it was still a guitar.

Juni gave the strings a little strum. He locked eyes with his sister. And once again, a silent communication passed between them.

Ready for a fight? Juni asked Carmen with his eyes.

Totally, Carmen answered. She folded up the self-flaming stick, extinguishing its glowing ember. The cave went pitch-black. The only scanty source of light was the flashing from O. Zohn's fingertips.

"What are you doing?" O. Zohn bellowed from across the cave. "You can't hide from the powers of the Atmoso Amulet!"

"Hurry," Carmen hissed to her brother. She reached into her spy bag and grabbed O. Zohn's Hypn-O-Nar. She slipped it to Juni, who used a scrap of lanyard string to lash it to his guitar.

"Cover your ears," Carmen whispered to Cecilia, slapping her own palms over her ears.

"Why?" Cecilia squeaked.

"Just do it!" Carmen hissed.

And then, Juni began to play a dorky folk song.

"I gave my love a chicken," he began singing, "that had no bone . . . "

"What's that?" O. Zohn's voice rang out through the dark cave. More lightning bolts flashed. "Why are you singing?"

"I gave my love an ice cream," Juni warbled, "that had no cone . . . "

"Shut up!" O. Zohn cried.

But Juni persisted.

"I gave my love a sheep," he sang.

"Stop it," O. Zohn shrieked. "I *hate* folk music! I never want to hear another folk song again. I only sang those songs to hypno . . . hypno . . . tize. . . . "

Juni stopped strumming.

And Carmen pulled out the self-flaming stick again. When the ember lit the cave, she saw that O. Zohn had a dreamy look on his face. He was smiling sweetly at Juni.

"I want you to give me the Atmoso Amulet," Juni ordered the camp director.

With another agreeable grin, O. Zohn took the amulet off and handed it to the Spy Kid. Juni handed his guitar to Carmen and walked to the niche in the wall. He placed the Atmoso Amulet onto its silk pillow.

The amulet began to spark. And sputter. It shot blue flames up toward the ceiling! And then, it melted into a fizzy, golden puddle!

"Whoa!" Juni cried. "Replacing the amulet must have broken the curse and destroyed it. Bonus!"

"Perfect!" Carmen said with a grin. She unlooped the lanyard strings from Juni's makeshift guitar. Then she wrapped the strings around and around O. Zohn's slack wrists and ankles. In under a minute, he was completely cuffed.

Carmen dusted off her hands.

"Okay, Cecilia," she said as she glared at O. Zohn. "As a Level Four, you've probably never made an arrest. Watch and learn . . . Cecilia?"

Carmen glanced at the young Spy Kid behind her. Cecilia was completely ignoring her. Instead, she simply gazed dreamily at Juni.

"Cecilia?" Carmen said. "Did you cover your ears like I told you to?"

"Huuuuh?" Cecilia asked woozily. Then she batted her eyelashes at Juni.

Juni gaped back at her. Then he slapped his forehead.

"Oh no!" he cried. "I've hypnotized Cecilia. That's like a crush squared! She's *never* gonna leave me alone, now!"

Carmen laughed.

"Well, look at the sunny side," she said. "The Atmoso Amulet is a thing of the past. Our evil camp director is going to be behind bars as soon as we call the OSS. *And* we won the Spy War!"

"In other words . . . " Juni said with a grin.

" . . . we totally saved the world," Carmen crowed. "Again!"

CHAPTER 17

The next few days at Camp Spy Valley were a whirlwind. But a *good* kind of whirlwind.

First, Carmen and Juni called the OSS headquarters and debriefed the agency about their mad—but conquered—camp director. Within minutes, two OSS helicopters swooped into Spy Valley.

One helicopter was used to haul the evil O. Zohn off to jail.

And from the other emerged a pretty woman with a blond ponytail and long, tanned legs. Right behind her was Devlin, the cleft-chinned, rakish head of the OSS.

"Carmen, Juni," Devlin said, shaking hands with the Spy Kids. "I'd like to personally thank you for saving the world. Again!"

"Just doing our job, Mr. Devlin," Carmen said, a bit wearily.

"Well, even spies should be rewarded for a job well done," Devlin replied.

"Cool!" Juni said. "How about letting us go home? That would be an excellent reward!"

Devlin and the blond woman exchanged a glance. Then the woman bent down and looked Juni, then Carmen, in the eye.

"I'm Jane Goodmall," she said. "OSS spy and new director of Camp Spy Valley."

Carmen and Juni gave each other a dubious look.

"Is there anything I could do to convince you to give Spy Valley another try?" Jane asked. "I was thinking we could start off with a big cookout in the clearing tonight."

Juni's eyebrows shot up. He gave Carmen another glance. A . . . hopeful glance. She shrugged and nodded.

"I guess we could be persuaded," Carmen told the pretty woman.

And thus began a whole new feeling at Camp Spy Valley. Over the next few days, the campers' bruises began to fade and their spirits soared. They caught up on their sleep and began to actually have fun!

"Announcements, an-NOUNCE-ments, an-NOUNCE-ments! Time for campfire with your camp director, Jane Goodmall. And remember, BYOM!"

"Yes!" Juni said. He grabbed a plastic bag from his cubby and hurried to the clearing in front of the lodge. As he ran, he spotted Cecilia.

"Oh, brother," he muttered. He was just about to duck behind a tree to avoid her when he saw that Cecilia wasn't walking alone. She was with Toby.

In fact, Cecilia and Toby were *holding hands*!

"Cecilia!" Juni blurted in surprise.

"Oh . . . hi, Juni," Cecilia said uncomfortably as Juni walked up to her and Toby. "What's up?"

"Oh . . . nothing," Juni said. He shrugged sheepishly. Then he kicked at the grass. And then, before he could stop the words from escaping his lips, Juni burst out, "What's the big idea, Cecilia? I thought you had a crush on *me*!"

Cecilia cringed again.

"I did," she said with a shrug. "But what can I say, Juni? When you weren't interested, I had to move on. And you know . . . "

Cecilia gave Toby a flirty glance.

" . . . intelligence can be so attractive in a boy!"

The statement made Toby turn bright red. Then he giggled so hard, his glasses fell off. Cecilia grabbed them off the grass and handed them back to Toby.

"Here ya go," she said.

"Thanks," he said, pushing the glasses up on his nose. Then he held out his hand to Juni. "Sorry, Juni. That's the way the cookie crumbles. Or as I like to say, that's the way the microchip coalesces into a binary-code reaction formation."

Juni blinked at Toby blankly. But then he shrugged and shook the young boy's hand.

"Hey, it's okay," he said. "The best man won."

This made Toby blush and snort with laughter again. Then he and Cecilia made their way to a cozy spot next to the campfire.

Juni continued trudging toward the fire. He was feeling strangely . . . bummed! What was up with that? After all, he'd wanted to unload that squeaky Cecilia from day one!

Juni was on the verge of pondering some life issues. Things like girls and growing up and stuff. But then Carmen bounded up to his side.

"I love BYOM night!" she said.

In an instant, Juni's brooding thoughts flew out of his head. He looked at the plastic bag, still clutched in his hand, and grinned.

"Bring Your Own Marshmallows," he said. "It's the best!"

Juni forgot all about Cecilia and Toby as he speared six of his marshmallows on a stick. Sitting next to Carmen on a fallen log, he began toasting the sweets over the big fire.

As the happy, well-rested campers toasted, munched, and chatted, Jane Goodmall joined the circle and waved her hands. Her fingertips were flashing and blinking like fireflies!

"Looks like I drank the wrong bug juice," she said with a laugh. "I'm still new at this camp director thing. But hey, at least it got your attention!"

Good-natured laughter rippled through the group. Jane was the coolest!

"I have one announcement to make before we get into full s'mores mode," Jane said. She pulled a clipboard off her belt and said, "As you all know, we had a cliff-climbing relay race today—excellent training for all the Spy Kids leaving on that Himalayan mission after the camp session ends. Now, I'd like to announce the winners of that race."

Jane paused dramatically. Then she called out, "The winners are Team Number Four, otherwise known as Delta Schmelta. Also otherwise known as Carmen, Beth, Cheryl, and Farrah of Beta Cabin."

"Yes!" Carmen cried, hopping to her feet. She and her teammates jumped up and down and hugged one another as Jane pinned blue ribbons to their shirts.

"I just want to say . . . " Farrah began.

"No, *I* want to say," Cheryl cut in, "that we couldn't have won this race without the stellar leadership of Carmen Cortez. She rocks!"

"Speaking of," Jane said, "I'd like to sing our winners a little song."

Jane reached behind a log and pulled out a guitar. Carmen shot Juni a panicked look.

Juni almost dropped his marshmallows! Instead, he shoved them into his mouth, then slapped his hands over his ears.

Twaa-aaa-aaaang!

Juni's mouth dropped open. Luckily, he'd swallowed his sweets. Jane was playing an *electric* guitar! And now, she was banging out some killer rock and roll!

"I can't get no," Jane sang, "OSS action! I can't get no, spying factions. But I try . . . "

Before long, the campers all jumped to their feet. And then they started dancing! And laughing! And singing along with the coolest camp director ever!

A very cute Delta boy was just shimmying up to Carmen when she heard someone call her name.

Someone with a deep voice.

And a Spanish accent!

"Dad?" Carmen cried. Over the bouncing heads

of her fellow Spy Kids, she saw her Dad at the edge of the clearing! Mom was standing right next to him. Their supertanned faces were furrowed with worry.

Carmen grabbed Juni and pointed at their parents. Then the Cortez kids ran across the clearing and threw themselves into Mom's and Dad's arms.

"We missed you!" Carmen cried. "But . . . what are you doing here? The camp session doesn't end for another two weeks."

"Well, of course, we jumped on a plane as soon as the OSS faxed us in Costa Rica!" Mom said. She put a warm hand on Carmen's cheek. "We were so worried! What's this about your camp director being an evil madman who used all the Spy Kids to track down a weather-controlling amulet?"

"Oh, that's so three days ago," Juni scoffed. "Don't worry. We saved the world."

"Again!" Carmen said with a grin.

"And then, the OSS sent us a new camp director," Juni said. He pointed at the blond woman dancing near the campfire. "Jane Goodmall. She's the one on lead guitar."

"Oh," Mom said, blinking in surprise.

"Oh," Dad said. "So, I guess we didn't need to leave our vacation after all."

"Sorry about that," Juni said.

"You could head back to Costa Rica in the morning," Carmen suggested.

"That's okay," Mom said with a shrug. "To tell you the truth, we really weren't having that much fun. We missed you too much!"

"Yes, it is true," Dad said, tousling Juni's curls. "OSS missions are no good without you kids."

Carmen and Juni exchanged a worried glance.

"What's wrong?" Mom and Dad asked together.

"Mom, Dad?" Carmen said. "Don't you ever wish your parenthood was more . . . normal?"

"Normal?" Mom stared at her children blankly. "You mean, the way we used to be?"

"Lame!" Dad protested.

"I'm sorry," Juni said with a gleam in his eye and a wink at his sister. "But you need to have some fun. You and Mom are going to continue your vacation. And Carmen and I are *staying* at camp."

Carmen nodded with a grin and said, "I agree. Case closed!"